CATHERINE GEORGE

silent crescendo

Harlequin Books

TORONTO • NEW YORK • LONDON
AMSTERDAM • PARIS • SYDNEY • HAMBURG
STOCKHOLM • ATHENS • TOKYO • MILAN

Harlequin Presents first edition April 1986
ISBN 0-373-10873-7

Original hardcover edition published in 1985
by Mills & Boon Limited

"Do you have to be so dramatic, Rafael?"

Judith regarded him thoughtfully. "I have this feeling you're following a libretto every now and then—it's very disconcerting."

To her surprise there was no answering smile. "I am sorry," he said in a monotone. "I had no desire to speak of this. But I am not the noble, silent type, Judith. For more than half my life I have made my living by expressing emotions through my voice, showing what I feel, suppressing very little. I do not want now to burden you with my problem."

"What problem?" she asked as she crossed the kitchen to him, suddenly desperate.

He shrugged. "The operation has done permanent damage to my throat. I can speak, but I cannot sing."

CATHERINE GEORGE was born in Wales, and following her marriage to an engineer lived eight years in Brazil at a gold mine site, an experience she would later draw upon for her books. It was not until she and her husband returned to England and bought a village post office and general store that she decided to try her hand at writing. With her husband's encouragement, she submitted her first book and was quickly accepted. Now her husband helps manage their household so that Catherine can devote more time to her writing. They have two children, a daughter and a son, who share their mother's love of language and writing.

Books by Catherine George

HARLEQUIN PRESENTS
800—PRODIGAL SISTER
858—INNOCENT PAWN
873—SILENT CRESCENDO

HARLEQUIN ROMANCE
2535—RELUCTANT PARAGON
2571—DREAM OF MIDSUMMER
2720—DESIRABLE PROPERTY

CHAPTER ONE

THE last of the dog-walkers had gone. The park was almost deserted, only a lone running figure in sight. Long hair flying, a girl sped with fluid, easy strides along a bridlepath leading up to a ridge crowned with a copse of oak and beech, the leaves stencilled soot-black against the darkening, gilt-edged sky. The half-light was eerie, and Judith quickened her pace, anxious to pass through the barrier of trees to reach the final downward stretch to the park gates. Close to the town though it was, Abbey Park was not the best of places to run alone at dusk, and gritting her teeth she increased her speed as she breasted the rise. Eyes distracted for an instant from force of habit to the floodlit clocktower of the church in the distance, Judith's breath was suddenly knocked from her body as she collided with an unseen runner hurtling out of the wood in the opposite direction.

With a muffled scream Judith landed on her back on the hard-packed earth, half winded by the body pinning her to the ground. She fought instinctively to be free, hair escaping from the sweatband round her forehead to blind her for a moment of breathless panic before she managed to struggle to her feet. Pushing the hair away from her eyes she stood transfixed, petrified, all her fears realised as she stared for a split-second of nightmare at the man in front of her. Tall, dressed in black, a ski-helmet over his face with holes for eyes and nose, he was the very stuff bad dreams are made of, and as he made a move towards her Judith came abruptly to life, letting fly with her fist to connect with a hard, wool-covered jaw. More by luck than skill the blow caught the man off-balance and Judith promptly took off, running like the wind down to the gates, pausing only long enough to open one and slide through, her breath tearing through her chest in painful gasps as she threw a look over her shoulder to see if the man were following her. He was not. He stood exactly where she had left him, a sinister shadow merging with the trees, and with an incredulous sob of relief Judith raced away down the long curve of Abbey Road and turned the corner into Chantry Lane. Halfway along the short row of houses the lights were on in Chantry Cottage and she slowed wearily to a walk, lifting the knocker as she reached the door, too spent even to search in her pocket for the key.

The door opened on the trim figure of her sister, who stood looking at her in disapproval. In contrast to Judith's dishevelment Honor was her usual immaculate self in silk shirt and linen skirt, smooth fair hair neatly coiled above her calm, beautiful face. Judith staggered past her into the kitchen, too shattered to care about her wild appearance as she tried to get her breath back.

'Where on earth have you been? I was worried—heavens, what's the matter?' Honor's disapproval swiftly changed to concern as Judith collapsed on one of the stools at the small breakfast bar in the kitchen, leaning her head in her hands as her breathing gradually slowed to normal.

'A man—in the park——'

'What!' In consternation Honor jerked Judith's head up and examined her flushed face closely. 'Did he hurt you? I've warned you about running in the park alone. Where was Rob? Did this man attack you, or—or anything?'

'No anything.' Judith managed a grin. 'He didn't really attack me either; we just had a collision by the copse of trees at the top of the hill. We landed in a heap, then I hit him on the jaw and scarpered. He looked utterly terrifying—all in black, with one of those balaclava things over his head with holes for eyes. I'm sad to say I panicked like mad and ran for it.'

Honor listened thoughtfully, her eyes troubled. 'Should we tell the police?'

'Tell them what? That I bumped into a man in Abbey Park? Not much, really, is it?' Judith got up to rummage in one of the drawers for a piece of string. 'It was probably just me being fanciful. I found myself alone in the park, it was almost dark and I had a shock. Maybe the man was more frightened than me!' She tied back her untidy hair with a frayed piece of cord.

'Did he say anything?'

'Not a word—just a sort of grunt when we collided. Don't worry—I'm sure he was just an ordinary jogger.'

'Only dumb, and wearing a woollen ski-cap over his head on an August evening,' said Honor tartly.

Judith shrugged and unzipped her track-suit top.

'Earache, maybe.'

'Or something!' Honor was sceptical. 'Have a shower, you look a wreck. I've no doubt all this excitement was on top of a game of squash?'

'Two, actually.' Judith gave her a guilty grin. 'Which is why I was so late. Rob's on call, by the way. I'm not seeing him tonight.'

'Right. Then we can eat at our leisure and I'll tell you all the news—it's been quite a day for me, too.'

'Don't say Arts Week has been cancelled!'

Honor shrugged her shoulders and stooped to inspect the contents of the oven. 'You're not so very far off the mark, as it happens. Get a move on, dinner's just about ready, so not another word until you're respectable.'

Judith was hungry after all her excitement, and hurried through her shower, not bothering to dry her thick russet-brown hair. She plaited it into a long rope, pulled on a sweatshirt and shorts and ran down to enjoy the chicken casserole Honor had waiting.

'So what's new, Honor?' she asked as they began to eat. 'Martin giving you trouble?'

'*Mr* Gresham never gives me trouble,' stated Honor with dignity. 'Clive Morrison is the problem.'

'What's up with our leading tenor, then?'

'Laryngitis,' said Honor tersely. 'He caught cold canoeing on, or rather *in* the river, and now his voice has gone. Totally irresponsible—I mean who could be so brainless as to risk half-drowning himself a few days before singing the lead in an opera!'

'Clive Morrison, obviously.' Judith looked at Honor in enquiry. 'No understudy?'

'Well, Mr Soames, the curate, *can* sing the part, but his upper register is a bit suspect, and apart from being several inches shorter than Meryl he finds it embarrassing to seethe with passion, being a man of the cloth and all that.'

Judith tried hard to keep a straight face, but failed, and giggled despite the quelling hazel turned on her. 'Sorry, Honor, but it *is* a bit comic you must admit!'

'Just because you haven't a note of music in you, Judith Russell, doesn't mean you can't appreciate the problem it is for Mr Gresham,' said Honor severely, but the corners of her mouth twitched involuntarily. 'A good thing you weren't at the rehearsal in the theatre this evening to see Mr Soames gazing up into Meryl's frozen face singing "O life of my life, do not shatter my heart" in the most extraordinary Italian!'

'Oh I wish I had been,' said Judith fervently. 'What did Martin Gresham have to say about that?'

'He wasn't there. The trouble blew up yesterday. I went to bed before you got in last night and I went out this morning before you got up, so I haven't had a chance to tell you. Mr Gresham went dashing off to London when he heard the news about Clive, and I've been in the library all day today, but he rang me about four to say the problem was solved, but he didn't elaborate, so I don't know how.'

'Curiouser and curiouser!' Judith slid off the stool and put their plates into the sink. 'Any pudding, Honor?'

'Stewed plums and cream in the fridge.'

After supper the two girls watched television for a while in the main room of the cottage. Two smaller rooms had been knocked into one, with the original bow-window looking out on the street and another, larger and newer, giving on to the small patio garden at the back. The furniture was simple; chintz-covered chairs, one or two good pieces like the writing desk and the sofa table, and there were some pleasing flower prints on the plain, cream-washed walls. Chantry Cottage had been Honor's first home when she married Simon Gregg ten years previously. The marriage had been sadly brief. Simon dying prematurely from a heart attack, and afterwards, in spite of much opposition from her family Honor had insisted on keeping on her little house, preferring to stay in Hardwick, the Midlands market town where she had made a life for herself, rather than live with her parents again, much as she loved them.

Judith's friends had scoffed at her when she chose to work in the Hardwick Memorial Hospital after qualifying as a physiotherapist from the Nuffield, telling her she was wet behind the ears to choose the town where her sister lived. Judith had gone one better and taken up Honor's offer of a room, an arrangement which had turned out surprisingly well despite, or possibly because of, the nine year difference in age. After years of living in hall and then a student flat, not to mention the eccentricity of the family home, Honor's neat, pretty little house was different; ordered and well run, with no intrusion on privacy on either side, as Judith was given the larger upstairs room to arrange as her own bed sitting-room where she could have friends round, or take herself off when Honor entertained friends of her own.

Tonight, after the disturbing experience in the park, Judith was very glad of her sister's calm presence, grateful just to relax and chat with Honor. Judith invariably played squash on her day off, and it was her habit to run back through the park again afterwards, but always much earlier, when there were plenty of people about, unlike this evening. Not given to nerves much as a rule she was frankly shattered by her encounter, which came into the category of things that happened to other people, not to Judith Russell. She dismissed the incident from her mind and got up to make coffee for them both. It was actually quite rare for the two girls to spend an evening alone together. Honor was a librarian, and spent most of her free time working for Martin Gresham, Arts Director of the Hardwick Arts Society, while Judith had a steady escort in the burly shape of Dr Robert Bailey, a G.P. with one of the town medical practices. He was a member of the same club where they liked to exercise regularly, or play squash when they had enough energy left over from the demands of their respective professions.

'The thing is, Honor,' said Judith, as she brought back a tray from the kitchen, 'won't Arts Week be adversely affected if the opera is cancelled? I rather thought it was the high point of the week.'

'It is—or was,' sighed Honor. 'Not that it's as ambitious as it sounds, actually. It's only the third act of *La Rondine*, and a concert version at that, not the whole operatic bit. The first half of the evening is just a normal concert. I just feel so sorry for Mr Gresham. He's put such a lot of hard work into it, and this particular opera is his pet thing. No one else seems even to have heard of it before. It was the last one Puccini ever wrote—very lightweight and charming. Anyway, Mr Gresham seems to have the problem solved somehow.'

'Perhaps he's going to sing the lead himself,' suggested Judith. She grinned provocatively at Honor over her cup.

'Hardly!' Honor's eyes narrowed accusingly. 'Why do I always get the feeling you have something against Mr Gresham?'

'Only his myopia, darling!'

'He's not in the least short-sighted!' Honor set her cup down with a bang, the colour rising under her fine, fair skin. 'There's nothing wrong with his eyes.'

'Only that they can't see what's right in front of them,' said Judith bluntly. 'He's forty, divorced, highly solvent and not bad to look at either, if you like your men bony and brainy—and you obviously do. And you aren't so bad yourself—blonde, thirty-ish——'

'Thirty-four.'

'Like I said, thirty-ish, and a very attractive lady. And you're in love with him,' went on Judith relentlessly. 'So why doesn't he snap you up?'

Honor stared at her sister, appalled. 'Judith I am not in love with him——'

'Liar!'

'In any case, he's a Gresham of Hardwick. His family

practically owns the place, *and* they go back to the Conqueror, I shouldn't wonder. Why should he look at me, for heaven's sake.'

'Why not? If he's looking for a lady of quality he'll go a long way to do better.' Judith jumped to her feet, looking absurdly young in her brief shorts, the thick braid hanging over one shoulder. Her big dark eyes blazed with sincerity as she gave Honor a little shake. 'And not just because you're my sister, either. These are the eighties, woman. Apart from Crufts, who cares about pedigrees in this day and age?'

Honor frowned as Judith took the coffee tray to the kitchen. She was still deep in thought when Judith came back after washing up.

'Does it stick out a mile?' she asked quietly.

'No, of course not.' Judith dropped down on the floor, her back against the sofa. 'No one would notice except a busybody like me. And that's only because I've come to know you so much better this past year or so, Honor. In my opinion you're good enough for anyone—and heaven help you if Mother catches you saying otherwise!'

Honor laughed, her eyes clearing at the mention of their mother, who wrote gory, intricate whodunnits in the attic study of the Russell household near Abergavenny, where her father, retired from the Civil Service, strove to maintain some kind of order and peace over the rabidly nationalistic Welsh daily help, three cats, two dogs and the goats who cropped the grass in the paddocks adjoining the garden.

The next morning Judith set out briskly along the canal towpath that led past the hospital. With autumn in the offing it would soon be better to take the long way round through the outskirts of the town she decided regretfully. At the moment there were schoolboys fishing in groups along the canal bank and the occasional narrowboat cruised along, filled with holidaying families, but soon it would be deserted and lonely. Damn, thought Judith in exasperation. She had never given the loneliness a thought before, but after last night's little incident she seemed to be looking for prowlers behind every bush, and this was a cheerful sunny morning. Heaven help her when the weather was foggy and grey and the canal frankly sinister, as it could often seem during the winter months. She would just have to forget her silly qualms by then. Judith took herself firmly in hand, resolving never to think about the man in black again, which was easy once she reached the hospital. The moment she changed into her neat white tunic and dark blue trousers her attention was centred solely on the patients needing her ministrations. Tending to the breathing problems of road-accident victims Judith forgot herself entirely, her attention focused on helping people back to normal again as efficiently and sympathetically as she could. It was a busy, physically demanding day as always, particularly in the orthopaedic ward with some of the spinal injuries, and it was only when she found herself on the busy main roads of the town on the way home that she realised she had opted subconsciously for the safety of pavements rather than the lonely canal towpath.

Her footsteps faltered. This was silly. She was allowing one isolated incident to alter her entire outlook. Judith strode on through the town, annoyed with herself, oblivious to shop windows that normally tempted her to dawdle, intent on getting home to do something about dinner. The two women shared the cooking between them and Judith always organised the meal on Honor's late evenings at the library. Rob was coming round to join them, as he often did as a change from eating out, or the salads and takeaway meals he subsisted on in his own bachelor flat. Judith had bought gammon steaks and vegetables during her lunch hour and once she was home quickly set to work, slicing potatoes and onions in a casserole with a cheese sauce, putting the dish in the oven to cook while she sliced runner beans, washed mushrooms, made a salad, and put the gammon steaks on the grill pan ready to cook when the others arrived.

She was bathed and perfumed, her hair swept into a glossy waterfall on one side of her head, looking her vivid best in pink cotton trousers and pink and blue floral silk shirt when the doorbell rang. Rob stood on the doorstep, his fair, goodlooking face glum and depressed. Judith eyed his dark suit and hangdog look with resignation.

'Let me guess,' she said with a sigh. 'You're doing someone else's calls tonight. Have you time to come in?'

'Yes—for a while at least.' Rob followed her into the sitting room and flopped down on a chair, his legs stretched out in front of him. There were dark stains of weariness below his blue eyes and he yawned widely. 'Sorry, Judith—again. I've given your number to the practice. I said they could reach me here until seven—hope you don't mind.'

'No, of course not,' she said cheerfully. 'I'm afraid dinner's not ready, so what can I give you to keep you going—a sandwich and coffee?'

'Great,' he mumbled, eyes closed. 'Anything.'

Judith shrugged philosophically as she hastily assembled a cheese and salad sandwich and cut a slice of Honor's fruitcake. She made the coffee extra strong and carried the tray to the other room, where Rob lay sprawled asleep, snoring gently, his mouth open.

And they say romance is dead, thought Judith acidly. She nudged him awake and Rob came to with a start, hauling himself upright. He shook his head to clear it, blinking his eyes.

'Sorry, Judith.'

'You keep saying that, but you don't have to—I understand.'

'And I appreciate it,' he assured her, wolfing down his sandwich. 'Not every girl would, I know.'

'I can well believe that! What's the problem tonight?'

'Richards is still away on holiday, the other two are doing late surgery tonight, and George Bassett, who should be on call, is at his wife's bedside, cheering her on.'

'Amy's started labour?' asked Judith with interest. 'I'm due in the maternity ward tomorrow. I'll look in on her.'

Rob looked at her repentantly.

'I'm so damn tired I haven't told you how delectable you look—come here and give me a kiss.'

Judith eyed him coldly.

'Your timing is out, Rob Bailey. I'm no vainer than anyone else, but coming in a poor third after sandwiches and coffee is a bit of a turn-off.'

'Sorry—no, all right,' he amended hastily, 'I won't repeat myself.' He looked at her hopefully. 'I'm only on until ten. I could come back then.'

Judith shook her head firmly.

'By then all you'll be fit for is bed, Dr Bailey.'

'And I suppose it's no use asking you to join me in mine?' he asked, with the air of someone expecting instant refusal.

'Dead right, Rob. No use at all.'

Rob put down his cup and got to his feet, staring down at her moodily. Not very far down—he was almost six feet tall, but Judith stood five feet nine in her bare feet and her wide dark eyes met his steadily, almost on the same level.

'You don't object when I make love to you,' he said, aggrieved, 'at least, as much as you'll let me. So why won't you move in with me, Judy——'

'You know why. And don't call me Judy.'

'I know you say you're not ready. But I don't know why,' he persisted stubbornly. 'Honor lived here alone for years before you left college—she wouldn't object if you moved out, surely?'

'Probably not, but I would, Rob.' In his present state of weariness Judith had no intention of letting him embroil her in the old, well-worn argument. 'Let's not talk about it now, Rob, anyway. You're dead on your feet.'

'I'll take you to dinner at the Sceptre tomorrow night,' he promised, and reached out a hand to her smooth, olive-skinned cheek. He groaned as the telephone interrupted them. 'That's probably for me.'

It was. Judith left him answering the call and went to dispose of the tray with the remains of his snack. She could hear him answering in a suddenly brisk voice, which meant the medical man was back in control once more. Rob met her in the hall.

'I'm on my way, Judith,' he kissed her absently, his mind obviously on the patient needing him, and Judith patted his stubbly cheek.

'Bye, Rob. Take care. See you tomorrow.'

He was gone without a backward glance, and Judith washed his cup and plate, her mouth wry. She was used to this sort of thing, most of her men friends up to now had been in the medical profession, in one line or another. It was high time she met someone with a career that allowed him to think of other things occasionally. Rob was also very much inclined to talk shop during their time together, and it would be pleasant to have a companion slightly less wrapped up in his own particular calling—if such an animal existed.

As she was checking up on the casserole the telephone rang again. It was Honor this time.

'I hope you haven't gone to much trouble with dinner, Judith,' she began, sounding breathless and quite unlike her usual unflustered self.

'Not in the least,' Judith assured her. 'Where are you eating then?'

'Here, actually.'

'At the *library*?'

'No, no. They let me off early in fact, because Mr Gresham wanted me at Gresham House—I'll tell you all about it when I get home.'

'Is *that* where you're dining? Gresham House?'

'Yes! See you later, must go now.'

Eyebrows raised, Judith put two slices of gammon back in the refrigerator and began to grill the third. Her dinner partners might have fallen by the wayside, but her own healthy appetite was present and making itself felt. She cheerfully cooked herself a substantial meal and sat down in front of a television play to enjoy it. As she washed up afterwards she glanced up at the kitchen clock, wondering how Honor was getting along at Gresham House, which was a picturesque Palladian building in extensive grounds that bordered the west side of Abbey Park. Its owner, Martin Gresham, had been invalided out of the army a few years before, and now appeared content to administer his estate and interest himself in the affairs of the town. In Judith's opinion it was a pity he couldn't show more interest in the affairs of one Honor Gregg. It was high time her sister gave up being a widow and became a wife again—even a mother. There were no children from Martin Gresham's former marriage, and it seemed more than likely he would want a son to carry on his family name. She sighed. He might not care two hoots about a family, of course, but just the same she would dearly love to see Honor gain her heart's desire.

By the time the clock struck eleven Judith had trouble in keeping her eyes open. Her body was a beautifully-shaped, perfectly functioning piece of machinery, which demanded good food and eight hours' rest in return for the hard work and strenuous exercise its owner expected from it, and normally she was in bed and asleep well before midnight during the week. She yawned, switched off the television and stretched out on the small sofa. Honor was out late so seldom it seemed a bit churlish to go to bed before she came home, and with an effort Judith tried to concentrate on a complicated espionage story, but it was no use. Her eyes kept closing, her full mouth drooped, and with a sigh she eventually gave up and turned her head into the cushion, the book sliding to the floor.

She came to hazily, as Honor shook her awake in a state of excitement that jerked Judith upright in surprise.

'Judith, wake up! Judith, what do you think? You'll never guess what's happened——'

'No, I won't,' agreed Judith, rubbing her eyes sleepily. 'So tell me.' She looked curiously at her sister, who looked almost luminous with excitement.

'I had the surprise of my life when Martin asked me to come over to the house for dinner,' began Honor, poised on the edge of a chair.

'So it's "Martin" now!'

Honor brushed this aside impatiently.

'All the publicity handouts and posters have to be re-done—that's what we've been doing this evening, or

partly—and the printers have agreed to do a rush
job——'

'Hold on a minute! Just tell me why,' demanded
Judith, some of her sister's urgency rubbing off.

'Because, sister dear, Martin has found a replacement
to sing Clive Morrison's role in *La Rondine*!' Honor
gave a bubbling, youthful giggle. 'Though "replacement" hardly seems the right term. Guess who's
going to sing Ruggiero? Right here in the William
Gresham Theatre!'

'How do I know?' Judith asked, exasperated. 'Don't
keep me in suspense.'

'Only Rafael David himself!' announced Honor with
éclat.

'Is he the one who appears on television quite a bit?'

Honor cast her eyes heavenwards in despair.

'Honestly, Judith, you're the absolute end. Rafael
David only happens to be one of the world's leading
young operatic tenors, and all you can say is that he's
on television quite a bit! Considering how fanatic the
parents and I are about music I wonder sometimes
where you came from.'

'Perhaps I'm a changeling!' Judith grinned. 'Anyway
if the bloke wasn't on television at all I would never
have heard of him. I'm hardly the world's greatest
authority on opera. But, I didn't mean to prick your
balloon, love. It sounds marvellous—Hardwick will be
in uproar. When's he arriving?'

'He's already here. He arrived yesterday. He's taking
some time off—overdoing things a bit, I gather, and
came to stay with Martin. I actually had dinner with
Martin Gresham *and* Rafael David, Judith, can you
imagine it?'

'What did you have to eat?'

'Is that the only interest you can summon up, you
philistine?' Honor shook her head, laughing. 'Roast
lamb, if you must know, then we worked out the extra
rehearsal time necessary and I let the other principals
know. Meryl Moore, the soprano, nearly went into
orbit from shock. She was still babbling gibberish when
I put the 'phone down!'

Judith remembered something.

'Isn't the concert on Monday, Honor! That's only three days' rehearsal. Cutting it a bit fine, isn't it—much I know about it, of course.'

'Apparently Rafael David considers it more than enough. He knows the role well, the others certainly *know* theirs, so they just need to get it together.'

Judith got up, yawning.

'Well, I'm glad you're glad, love. Especially since you actually crossed the threshold of Gresham Place. What's it like?'

Honor's eyes took on a dreamy look.

'Beautiful. Not awe-inspiring; nothing of that museum atmosphere you get in some big houses. It's quite compact really, not as large as I'd expected.'

'So you had a great evening, Honor. I'm pleased. Was Martin a kind host?'

'Perfect.' Honor lapsed into silence for a moment, her eyes absent. She looked up suddenly at Judith, who was untying her mane of hair. 'You haven't asked me what he's like.'

'Well, I know what he's like,' said Judith reasonably. 'He seems like a very nice, charming man—not my type, I'll admit——'

'I'm not talking about Martin,' said Honor impatiently. 'I meant Rafael David, fresh from La Scala, the Met., Covent Garden, regarded by some as the finest interpreter of Verdi on the operatic stage!'

'Well, I've had a glimpse of him once or twice on television when you've been glued to some opera, but I don't remember much about him except that he was dark and foreign-looking, and he wasn't as podgy as the usual run of Italian tenors, I suppose.'

'I'm sure he'd be overjoyed to hear such enthusiasm,' said Honor drily, 'and just for the record, darling, he's not Italian, but half Spanish, half Welsh.'

Judith made a face.

'Pretty fearsome combination—anyway, I'm not so much interested in the ravishing Rafael as how you got on with Martin. Was he nice to you, my love?'

'Very.' Surprisingly Honor dimpled and looked

definitely pleased with herself. 'He rang the head librarian and asked if I could have time off, as he wanted me until Arts Week was over.' Impulsively she flung her arms round Judith and reached up to give her a smacking kiss. 'Now go to bed—you're out on your feet. I'm sorry to have kept you up so late.'

'Think nothing of it,' said Judith airily as they switched off lights and locked up. 'At least you can sleep soundly now with one happy thought in mind.'

'What's that?'

'The celebrated Mr David—or should one say Señor—is a dead cert to beat poor Mr Soames into a cocked hat as leading man!'

CHAPTER TWO

THE two girls saw very little of each other for the next few days, the odd meal snatched together the most they could manage. Honor was blissfully up to her ears in preparations for Arts Week and the concert, and Judith worked part of the weekend as well as her usual hours, all of which proved so hectic at the hospital she had very little energy left over in the evenings, which was unusual. Her normal working day quite often left her tired, but never quite so completely drained. One of her patients, a teenage victim of a road accident, had unexpectedly died during the week, which was a major part of her trouble, leaving her sick at heart at the terrible waste of a life.

In the two years since qualifying Judith had trained herself to become objective, to keep a sense of detachment, almost a toughness she found was just as necessary as compassion, and at first the contrast between the high academic training required to qualify and the practicalities of actual day by day hospital work with real live patients had needed tremendous adjustment. Usually she felt this had been achieved with considerable success. She was sensible, and she was

physically strong, and used her spare time to make sure
she kept her body in good shape. The latter was
undeniable. Her square-shouldered, slim-hipped body
was beautiful, with high, full breasts, a slim waist, and
legs that went on forever, as Honor said enviously. She
had clear, smooth skin and dark, almond-shaped eyes
which sparkled with good health, combined with a
straight nose above a generously curved mouth. But for
the moment some of the glow was diminished, dimmed.
Rob was a little anxious when she declined a drive into
the Cotswolds for a meal when he came round on
Saturday night.

'Not sickening or anything, Judith?' he asked at once,
running a professional eye over her.

'No. Just a bit tired. Would you mind if we just sat
here and lazed in front of the television, Rob? Honor's
out at Gresham House again, or up at the theatre,
submerged in all the Arts Week hubbub, so we have the
place to ourselves.'

Rob gave her rather a crooked smile and drew up a
chair near the sofa where she lay full length. 'I wish I
could interpret that as some sort of invitation, but I
know better. What's up? Job depressing you?'

'A bit. Don't worry, I'll get over it. I'll rustle up
something for us to eat in a minute.'

'No. Stay where you are—I've a better idea.' He
jumped up, smiling down into her questioning face. 'I'll
nip out and raid the nearest takeaway merchant I can
find. Let's have something really sinful and unhealthy!'

Judith laughed. 'O.K. You're the doctor. We still
have the bottle of wine you brought last week, so we'll
have a picnic in front of the most mindless programme
the box can offer.'

They spent a pleasant, undemanding evening together
consuming butterfly prawns and fried rice and Rob's
favourite spring rolls, washed down with wine and
followed by slices of a chocolate cake intended by
Honor for Sunday tea.

'She won't mind,' insisted Judith, licking her fingers,
'unless I keep her awake with galloping indigestion.
She's floating around on her own personal little pink

cloud these days . . .' She stopped guiltily, not wanting to discuss Honor's secret *tendre* for Martin Gresham.

'Because this tenor chap is taking over at the concert?' Rob chuckled. 'The whole town is agog. Apparently there's even a black market in tickets. Gresham could have sold the place out three times over, I hear. Not to me, mind—more the David Bowie type myself.'

'M'm,' said Judith absently, looking up the television programme in the paper. 'Want to watch the cricket highlights?' She got up to change channels and took the greasy debris of their meal into the kitchen. 'I've got a ticket myself, by the way,' she said as she came back and sat down.

'What for?'

'The celebrity concert, of course. Not my cup of tea at all, especially as the opera they're putting on is some obscure piece I've never heard of. Not that I'm exactly wild over the famous ones, either.'

'The local paper was full of pictures of this chap as Don José, in *Carmen*. Apparently his is the definitive version of the role, whatever that means.' Rob came to sit beside her and took her hand.

'I saw someone else doing that in some dreary version on television not so long ago with Honor.' Judith smiled. 'I didn't see much of it, but to me Don José seemed like a knife-slinging wimp in a fancy uniform.'

'I suspect that's sacrilege to some people, Miss Russell—not that I care! Cuddle up and kiss me; let the doctor make you better.' Rob pulled her into his arms and began to kiss her with determination. Judith let him for a while, doing her best to match his enthusiasm, but it was no use. Try as hard as she could she remained obstinately aware of the arm of the sofa prodding her in the back, the faint lingering aroma of their meal and a definite sharp recoil when Rob's tongue thrust into her mouth as his fingers fumbled with the buttons of her dress. She drew back abruptly and pushed him away.

'No! Sorry—I'm just not in the mood.'

Rob jumped to his feet, flushed and angry, his blue eyes resentful.

'Just when are you likely to *be* in the mood, Judith? Shall I make an appointment for Wednesday week, say, or maybe even that's a bit soon for you.' He flung away, thrusting his fingers through his fair hair, staring angrily at the television.

Judith sighed and got up, putting a conciliatory hand on his shoulder, but he shook it off irritably and reached down for his jacket on the chair.

'I'm sorry,' she said tentatively. 'I feel a bit under par tonight, that's all'

'And what will the reason be next time?' he asked bitterly. 'That old standby the headache?'

'If that's the mood you're in,' she snapped, 'you might as well leave.'

'I'm going! Perhaps there'll be more congenial company at the club.' He stood glaring at her.

'Fine. You do that.' Judith stood tall and unyielding, meeting his glare head on, and with a muttered oath young Dr Bailey flung out of the room and charged out of the cottage, banging the door behind him.

Judith flopped down again on the sofa, annoyed with herself, conscious she had handled the incident rather badly. If Rob's advances had been nipped in the bud a little earlier he would have taken it like a lamb as usual, but an attempt to work up some feeling in herself had only succeeded in working up a great deal too much in him, poor man. He could hardly be blamed for turning vicious. She sighed. A strange sort of week this had been—dating from her collision with the sinister figure in the park, to be accurate. The weird thing had been, underlying the shock and terror, a totally irrelevant awareness of the scent of the man who had cannoned into her with such force. Some microscopic part of her brain had taken time to register a musky fragrance, aromatic, but sharp, as though the heat of his body had mingled with some kind of cologne. Which was utter fantasy, Judith informed herself tartly. The entire incident had taken only seconds, with no time to think of scents. If there had been anything it had probably been the scent of her own fear.

Restless and out of sorts, lost for something to do,

Judith finally resumed the book abandoned previously, and forced herself to keep her attention on it until Honor returned from the rehearsal. When her sister eventually arrived she came in glowing, her fair, delicate face surprised when she saw Judith was alone.

'You're in early for a Saturday night! Where's Rob?'

'He stormed off in a temper. We had a slight difference of opinion.' Judith avoided Honor's searching eyes and went out to the kitchen. 'Want some coffee?'

'Yes, please.' Honor took the pins out of her swathe of fair hair, yawning.

'How did it go tonight?'

'Wonderful. What a man!' Honor hesitated, then turned away quickly. 'I'm just going upstairs to get into my dressing gown and wash my face—I feel a wreck.'

When she came down again Judith had a tray ready with biscuits and coffee, and she smiled at Honor, who looked like a teenager with her face scrubbed clean beneath the fall of blonde hair, her feet bare below her blue cotton housecoat.

'Worn out with all this overdose of culture, sis?'

'Tired, but I'm enjoying it all enormously. I feel so privileged just to be at the rehearsals—what a voice this man has, Judith! He's electrified the rest of the cast completely. Meryl, in particular, is singing far better than I've ever heard her.'

'Something like playing squash with a professional—one plays up to his standard rather than the other way around.'

Honor looked at Judith searchingly.

'Didn't you go out tonight?'

'No. I just didn't feel like it, somehow.'

'Something wrong?'

'No. Not really.' Judith raised wry dark eyes and smiled cheerfully. 'I've had an odd few days this week, different from usual. Which goes for you, too, Mrs Gregg, one way and another. You won't know what to do with yourself once all this excitement is over.'

'The same thing I always do, I suppose.' A faint shadow clouded Honor's face and Judith cursed herself for spoiling her sister's mood. They both looked round in surprise as the doorbell rang. Judith got up to answer it.

'It's liable to be Rob, back to make it up,' she said as she left the room. She was wrong. It was Martin Gresham who stood on the doorstep, a look of apology on his fine-boned face, and Honor's handbag in his hand.

'Miss Russell?'

'Mr Gresham, come in,' said Judith quickly, and ushered him into the hall before he had a chance to refuse.

'I do apologise,' he said diffidently. 'It's very late, I know, but I thought Honor—Mrs Gregg might be anxious when she missed her handbag.'

'How very kind, Mr Gresham, and it's not at all late,' said Judith firmly, almost pushing him into the sitting room, where Honor was in her bare feet, her cheeks bright pink as she pushed at the hair streaming over her shoulders. Martin Gresham stopped short at the sight of her, clearly taken aback.

'Mr Gresham's brought your handbag, Honor,' said Judith, as obviously no one else was about to say anything.

'How—how thoughtful,' said Honor breathlessly. 'Won't you sit down—Martin?'

Martin sat, apparently unable to drag his eyes from the sight of Honor *en déshabillé*. He recollected himself hurriedly as he realised Judith was offering him coffee.

'Why thank you. Yes. I would.'

Judith whisked herself out of the room and closed the door, taking as long as she possibly could to make another pot of coffee, washing up the glasses and cutlery from earlier on while she was at it to give Honor more time with Martin. Feeling rather like some trainee fairy godmother she finally went back to the other room to find Honor chatting away quite happily, completely at her ease. Martin looked distinctly captivated and almost had to tear himself away from contemplation of Honor's bare feet when his innate good manners prompted him to include Judith in the conversation, questioning her about her work in the hospital, and whether she were coming to the opening concert of the Arts Festival.

'I have a ticket, of course,' she said, smiling, 'but from what I hear I might do better financially to put it up for auction. I gather the demand for seats has been fierce.'

'Once the word was out that Raf was appearing it was inevitable.' Martin looked across apologetically at Honor. 'I'm afraid I've let you in for a great deal more hard work than I intended, Honor.'

'I'm loving every minute of it,' she assured him, smiling happily.

'How does he happen to be staying with you, Mr Gresham?' asked Judith curiously. 'Hardwick seems like such a backwater for a man like Rafael David.'

'He's been coming here to stay with me for years, unknown to the general public,' Martin told her, 'We met as boys when I was travelling through Spain on holiday before I entered Sandhurst. He ran me down in his sports car in one of those steep streets in Granada, to be precise, and took me home to his mother's house. I wasn't injured in the slightest, but Doña Carmelita insisted on my staying with them for the rest of my holiday. She had just retired from the operatic stage at that time, and I was a diversion, she said—something to relieve her boredom. She was Carmelita Valentin, a mezzo soprano in the great Spanish tradition—Lord.' He stopped, embarrassed. 'I'm boring on at great length, and it's well past midnight. I should go.' He finished his coffee quickly and stood up.

'It's a fascinating story,' said Honor gently. 'Presumably he returned the compliment and came to stay with you afterwards?'

'Yes, exactly. That was before he was swallowed up in training at the Conservatory and on the stage. But afterwards we always managed to see each other as often as possible. His mother died years ago, unfortunately.'

'I'm very grateful to you for troubling to bring my handbag.' Honor smiled at him serenely.

'I was afraid you might worry, or that there was something you might need for tonight.'

'I would have needed my glasses to read the Sunday papers in the morning,' she said, with a little laugh.

Judith could have murdered her.

'Yes, of course, I usually see you in glasses,' Martin said absently, gazing down at Honor, obviously wondering whether this made the difference.

'I'm long-sighted,' Honor added, to make sure he understood.

Judith ground her teeth impotently in the background.

'One would never know it,' Martin assured Honor gravely. 'You have such lovely eyes.'

At once the colour came rushing back into Honor's face and she looked away in confusion. Bravo, applauded Judith silently, and was as charming as she knew how as she saw Martin Gresham to the door.

'I'm very glad to have met you, Miss Russell,' he said as he made his farewells. 'Of course you're coming to the party on Monday night, I hope—no doubt your sister has told you about it.'

'How kind, Mr Gresham,' said Judith a little blankly, and raced back to Honor in excitement the moment the door was closed. 'What a turn up for the books, love,' she chortled. 'Fancy his coming back just when you'd slipped into something more comfortable as they say. He was transfixed!' She halted at the look of guilt on Honor's face.

'It wasn't exactly a coincidence, Judith. I hoped—I mean, well, I rather planned the whole thing.' Honor bit her lip in remorse.

'Did you now!' A wicked smile of delight dawned in Judith's eyes.

Honor nodded glumly. 'I left the bag behind in his car deliberately. Then I rushed in and changed and took my hair down just in case he found it and brought it back.'

'And he did, he did,' crowed Judith, hugging her. 'It worked like a charm. But what on earth made you go on about wearing glasses, you cuckoo?'

'Conscience. I felt bound to remind him of how I look normally.'

'Which only served to emphasise how tempting you look when you're ready for bed!'

'Judith!'

'I'm right,' said Judith unrepentantly. 'It was one cliché after the other, you little schemer. The entire Hollywood bit, just like those old black and white movies on television in the small hours, where the hero slowly takes off the heroine's glasses and breathes "God—you're beautiful"—only you did it by inference, clever thing.'

Honor stared at her, looking troubled, then her lips twitched and she began to chuckle, and they both clutched each other and laughed until the tears came, Judith eventually recovering enough to demand information about the party.

'When, where and what, Honor? You're holding out on me!'

'Martin's throwing a party backstage after the concert for the performers and the Mayor and various notables, and the Russell girls are invited!'

It was only later that Judith realised the significance of the term 'Russell girls'. It seemed that at long last Honor was ready to think of herself as an eligible woman again, rather than poor Simon Gregg's widow.

To Judith's surprise and pleasure she and Honor had been invited to join Martin and his aunt, Miss Lavinia Gresham, in the family box, so she had raffled their tickets at the hospital, raising quite a large sum for toys for the children's ward as a result.

Hardwick Operatic Society was a well-organised affair, presided over by Ashley Moore, the choirmaster and organist of St Margaret's Church. His wife, Meryl, was singing Magda, the soprano lead in the excerpt from *La Rondine*, which was to take up the second half of the programme. Ordinarily Judith would have been bored to tears at the prospect of an evening spent listening to classical music of any kind, but tonight was different. The atmosphere in the packed theatre was

electric. In addition to the red plush elegance of the
usual seating Martin had strained fire regulations to the
limit by squeezing in more contemporary chairs all over
the auditorium, wherever there was the slightest
possibility of cramming them in, and all of them were
already occupied. Judith was very much aware of the
attention she and Honor were attracting, installed in
state in the Gresham box; both of them had taken great
pains with their appearance, Honor in a sheer Liberty
cotton dress with satin collar and cuffs, and Judith in
her favourite garnet red, silk and starkly plain. Miss
Gresham was obviously pleased to have their company,
and had made both girls affably welcome in a casual
way, waving them to the seats beside her. She was a
well-known figure in the town, prominent in the W.V.S.
and Women's Institute, and had lived with Martin since
his divorce. Eventually he took his place behind the
three women in the rather cramped confines of the box
just as the orchestra became quiet.

An expectant hush fell over the theatre. At the
opening bars of the National Anthem the audience rose
to its feet as one man, and from the corner of her eye
Judith had a glimpse of Martin, ramrod stiff to
attention while the orchestra played *God Save The
Queen*. It was an emotive beginning to an evening
already charged with excitement and anticipation, and
as the audience settled down again in a fluttering,
rustling buzz, Judith realised suddenly with surprise
that there was nowhere she would rather be at this
particular moment. She marvelled at the power and
talent of one man, who by his voice and personality
could command such a fanatical following, not only in
this particular audience, but wherever he appeared all
over the world.

The orchestra struck up the opening bars of the
Drinking Song from *La Traviata*, and the curtain rose
to reveal the entire operatic society in nineteenth
century evening dress as they sang the lilting, festive
music, and waltzed round the stage beneath glittering
chandeliers, the men's black and white costumes
contrasting with swaying crinolines in every colour of

the spectrum. Honor met Judith's eye and smiled, as if to say 'not so bad after all, is it?' and Miss Gresham beat time with her programme on the mahogany rail in front of the box, humming off-key rather audibly. It was a very good beginning, both as a spectacle and a pleasure to the ear, and the audience settled back, prepared to enjoy the rest of the evening to the full. They were not disappointed. The standard was both high and varied, from Meryl's version of the Laughing Song from *Die Fledermaus* to the Gypsy Dance from *Carmen*, performed with much verve and vigour by the girls of the local ballet school, the excitement heightened considerably by the superb performance of the young man on the timpani in the orchestra, his great shining drums pulsing through Bizet's well-known music like a throbbing in the veins. There was a roar of appreciation from the audience when the brilliantly clad girls collapsed exhausted on the stage at the final crescendo and the packed auditorium cleared to fill the various bars for drinks in the interval, everyone well pleased with the programme so far, but filled with even greater anticipation for what was to follow.

They were actually getting more for their money than expected, explained Martin as he led the three women through the crowd to a small table near the long windows at one side of the bar. A bottle of champagne stood waiting for them, and they all sipped with appreciation while Martin went on to elaborate. Since it was now Rafael David who was singing the role of Ruggiero in the opera it had been decided to present a cut-down version of both second and third acts, using the chorus as well as the principals.

'Raf did all the spadework with Ashley Moore,' explained Martin. 'He's an accomplished pianist, too, and sometimes does some composing himself, so it was no problem to cut the piece down to size. The entire company have thrown themselves into the revised version heart and soul—literally inspired to new heights by the presence of Raf, according to Ashley and Meryl.'

'He sounds like a sort of musical Superman,'

observed Judith, accepting a second glass of champagne.

Honor frowned at her. 'In just the brief time I've been in contact with him I rather think that's not a bad description, actually.'

'He's always been such an *energetic* boy,' said Miss Gresham affectionately. 'Never still a minute. I remember when he first came to stay when your parents were alive, Martin. What would he have been? Seventeen or so? On the go all day long; riding, swimming, tennis.'

Martin laughed reminiscently. 'We even used to put the gloves on and spar together, but I soon resigned from that—he grew too big for me to contend with.'

Judith was beginning to get very slightly bored with the name of Rafael David, and was rather glad when friends of the Greshams came to their table to pay their respects to Miss Gresham, patently curious about the presence of the two sisters. She joined in the general, light-hearted conversation with animation, and was almost sorry when the warning bell rang for the second half of the concert. She had a suspicion she was the only person in the entire building not looking forward much to the opera part, but was careful to keep her lack of enthusiasm to herself in case it smacked of ingratitude. The interval had been quite lengthy, and it was plain to see why when the curtain went up to the strains of lush, lilting waltz music to reveal a café scene with small tables at the front of the stage, with flower-starred hedges towards the back leading on to a realistic 'garden', where waltzing couples were laughing and singing, only half visible through the 'hedges', while a waiter served drinks to those seated at the tables out front. Gradually the audience became aware that the man sitting alone with his back to them was Rafael David. A great roar of applause broke out, and slowly the man got up, gravely bowing his acknowledgment of the tribute.

Judith scrutinised him with interst. The Gresham box was quite close to the stage, and Rafael David could be seen in detail. The thick black hair and aquiline, slant-

browed face were familiar enough from television, not
to mention the posters plastered all over town, but
photographs were no preparation for the sheer force of
the man's personality as he stood there waiting for the
applause to die down while the orchestra played a
reprise. Unlike the stiff evening dress of the other men,
Rafael wore a plain black suit with a loose jacket over a
frilled white shirt, a black silk scarf tied in a loose bow
at the open collar. The effect was vaguely bohemian,
suggestive of a costume rather than adhering to any
particular period, and suited his powerful physique. He
had the deep chest of the trained singer and stood well
over six feet tall, looking more like a heavy-weight
boxer to a surprised Judith, who secretly thought of
singers as rather an effete type of breed.

Eventually he seated himself at a table, the applause
died away and Meryl glided through the opening in the
'hedge', a china doll in a blue lace crinoline and blonde
ringlets. She approached the table where Rafael sat,
apparently asking if she might join him, though no one
took their eyes off the stage to consult the translation of
the libretto provided in the programme. *'Restate,
restate,'* he answered, and the singular power and
beauty of the renowned tenor voice took Judith by the
throat. She blinked, astonished at her own reaction, and
chanced a look at Honor, but her sister's eyes were
riveted to the stage as the magic unfolded. Meryl
Moore had a true, bell-like soprano voice, but in
response to Rafael David's it took on new depths and a
dramatic quality never suspected before. His voice,
however, was truly spectacular, Judith had to admit,
and he was no mean actor either; his whole demeanour
expressed a half-shy, half-ardent bemusement with the
girl beside him. As though she were the only thing in
life. Which must be quite odd for Ashley, Meryl's
husband, though presumably he could always wave his
baton threateningly from the podium if things got out
of hand. Judith smiled involuntarily in amusement, and
at the same moment Rafael looked up and caught her
eye. She moved her chair further back in the box in
embarrassment, and gave an apologetic shrug to Honor

when she frowned blackly in disapproval. No one else in the theatre was moving so much as an eyelash; everyone utterly still, hanging on every note, and gradually, insidiously, the enchantment began to overtake even Judith as the strong, lyrical voice wove a spell that rendered her defenceless against its allure. There was another short interval while the scenery was changed for the third act, but this time Judith sat silent in the bar while she listened to Martin's music-loving friends going on at some length about the 'red timbre of Rafael's voice' and 'the pride of the Spaniard combined with the mysticism of the Celt' in his ancestry.

'Tuneful little piece, dear, don't you think?' commented Miss Gresham, noting her silence. 'Fond of music, are you?'

'Not madly, Miss Gresham,' said Judith frankly. 'This is something out of the ordinary though, isn't it? Not an opportunity to miss.'

There was a shrewd twinkle in Lavinia Gresham's eyes.

'One consolation, Judith—if you don't care for the singing, Rafael's well worth looking at, you must admit?'

Judith laughed. 'Very true, Miss Gresham. It must be the experience of a lifetime for Meryl.'

'Ashley's wife? You're right. The lead in *Rose Marie* will seem a bit flat after this, poor gel.'

They chuckled together as they followed Honor and Martin back to the box. The orchestra was playing at full volume as they took their places, lowering almost to pianissimo as the curtain went up on Rafael and Meryl seated at a table with a painted vista of rolling lawns behind them, a suggestion of azure sea in the distance.

Judith no longer even tried to pretend she was unaffected by the music. A practical inner voice reminded her that this was very light opera indeed, not intended to be taken seriously, but it made no difference. She experienced a totally unexpected identification with what was happening on the stage, thrilling with Magda/Meryl when Ruggiero/Rafael took her in his arms, suffering when they were finally, inevitably forced to part at the end. Meryl drifted off-stage, casting a last look of anguish at Rafael, who knelt in mute pain, his bowed shoulders heaving, the last poignant strains of music died away and the curtain came slowly down. There was dead silence in the auditorium for a moment then the uproar began; applause, stamping feet, cries of 'bravo', the noise almost lifted the roof off the theatre. Judith applauded with everyone else, feeling dazed, even a little embarrassed at her total involvement in the music.

As the curtain rose the principals stood hand-in-hand in front of the chorus and bowed, and the clapping went on and on. Baskets of flowers were handed up on the stage, including a special offering of pink roses for Meryl, who was quite plainly somewhere only a little short of the stars with elation. Without hesitation she handed one to Rafael, who held it to his heart and kissed her hand with stylised grace, then with a sweep of her crinoline Meryl went to the front of the stage and held out the other bloom to her husband.

'Very proper, too,' approved Miss Gresham, as Rafael beckoned Ashley Moore up on the stage and signalled to the orchestra to rise to its feet in time-honoured fashion to receive their well-deserved share of the applause. Eventually Ashley held up his hands for silence and made a speech, thanking Rafael David for honouring the production with his presence, and thanking Martin Gresham for the organisation necessary behind the scenes, and then, with a smug little smile of satisfaction, informed the audience that they were to be given an extra, unexpected treat to round off the evening. Rafael David would sing a solo aria in response to the insistence of his old friend Martin Gresham. A few minutes' grace was requested, the curtain came down, Ashley returned to the podium and the audience sat back, hardly able to believe their good fortune.

When the curtain rose again Rafael stood alone on the stage. He had ruffled his hair a little, removed his jacket and swathed his black silk scarf round his waist. A silver knife was thrust through the sash, and in his hand he held a single red carnation. A sigh ran through the audience. By courtesy of Honor's television set even Judith knew what was coming next. At a stroke, the man on the stage was Don José, frustrated lover of Carmen the Gypsy. Quietly, softly, with immense control, he began the famous Flower Song. *'La fleur que tu m'avais jetée,'* he sang, staring at the flower in his hand, and even those without any knowledge of French at all had no difficulty in understanding the intensifying anguish and passion, mesmerised as he flung back his head at the end and sang, *'Carmen, Carmen, je t'aime'*.

This time, applaud as they might after the last plangent note died away, there were no more encores. The show was over at last, and Judith and Honor sat with Miss Gresham while Martin went behind the scenes to oversee the reception in preparation on the stage.

'Well?' demanded Honor, an odd smile on her face as she turned to Judith. 'Did you enjoy it after all?'

'Yes, I did.' Which was something of an under-statement. Judith felt drained.

'Is this your first experience of opera in the flesh, so to speak?' asked Miss Gresham. 'Your sister says you're the cuckoo in the nest, musically speaking.'

Judith nodded ruefully.

'I'm afraid Honor's right, Miss Gresham. But this performance was something out of the usual run tonight, wasn't it? The entire company did wonderfully well—at least they seemed to, to my untutored ear.'

The other two agreed with enthusiasm, and became engrossed in a discussion of the performance, which gave Judith a chance to excuse herself and slip away, conscious of a sudden, overpowering need to be alone for a minute or two. She went to the elegant, mirror-lined cloakroom and stared at herself in the mirror as she ran a perfunctory comb through her hair and straightened her dress, wondering why on earth she was possessed with an urge to go home, to avoid the party. Impatient with herself she added a touch of lipstick and rejoined Honor and Miss Gresham in the box, where Martin was waiting to escort them down to the stage.

Predictably Rafael David was surrounded by photo-
graphers and reporters, and submitted goodnaturedly
to being photographed with the Mayor, with Meryl,
then the entire cast, with Martin looking on good-
humouredly, but refusing to join the group himself.
After a look at his watch he eventually put an end to
the Press's attentions and courteously but firmly cleared
the stage of everyone except those entitled to be there,
and urged everyone to help themselves from the platters
of delicious cold food, and bottles of champagne which
waited on a long table covered with a white cloth.

For the first time in her life Judith felt rather shy. She
knew quite a few of the people there, but tonight the
common denominator was music and she felt alien, set
apart, despite Martin's good manners as he pressed
both sisters to the wine and food. The atmosphere was
fairly crackling with gaiety and celebration, everyone
connected with the concert riding high on a tide of
euphoria, including Honor, and Judith wanted very
much to leave her to Martin, and the rewards of her
hard work. She would have liked to stay with Miss
Gresham, but that lady was firmly enthroned in an easy
chair specially provided for her, and was holding court
with her own friends, which was only to be expected,
but left Judith feeling a little forlorn, excluded from the
magic circle that seemed to enclose everyone else.

'Judith, love, Martin wants me to meet a few people,'
said Honor anxiously. 'Will you be all right for a
minute?'

'Of course I will, big sister,' answered Judith lightly,
'I'm a big girl now. You trot off and do your own
thing—I'll be fine.' She watched Honor and Martin
affectionately as they moved away, then edged over to
the side of the stage, trying to make herself
inconspicuous among the scenery used for the first part
of the opera. She looked on from her shadowy corner,
sipping her champagne, amused at the way everyone
crowded around the famous tenor, wondering idly if he
were married; Martin had said nothing about a wife the
other night. Then she noticed the great man exerting his
not inconsiderable charm as he excused himself from

the people closest to him. To her surprise he collected a
champagne bottle from the table and turned purpose-
fully in what appeared to be her direction. Judith
glanced round her quickly, but no one else was
anywhere near. Rafael David was apparently making
straight for her, still dressed as Don José, stiletto and
all. Poser, thought Judith with mild scorn, and looked
at him without pleasure as he reached her side.

He made no attempt at a formal greeting. His face as
grave as hers he took her glass from her hand and filled
it carefully with champagne. 'Your glass was empty,' he
said, and bowed slightly as he handed it back to her.

Judith stiffened. The faint scent of his warm,
muscular frame was unmistakable; heated from his
recent exertions, his skin, combined with the cologne he
used, gave off a faint, familiar fragrance. She recognised
it immediately, and tensed.

'I have come to apologise,' Rafael went on, and
Judith stared at him in silence, momentarily bereft of
speech. 'I was the idiot who frightened you to death in
the park last week.' He took her hand, gazing down
into her startled eyes. 'Will you forgive me?'

'It was you!' she said at last, incredulous as her eyes
stared blankly into his. And what eyes he had. Not
black as she would have expected, but light amber, like
topazes, their brilliance framed by curling black lashes
any woman would have killed for.

'I am guilty,' he said softly, 'and also desolate to have
frightened you.'

Judith took her hand away hurriedly, conscious of
curious looks directed at them from all sides.

'I recovered,' she said evenly, 'though if you had
brought yourself to say something at the time it might
have helped.'

He gave a very Latin shrug. 'I was sworn to silence,
Miss—Miss——?'

'Russell.'

'Miss Russell. How do you do. I am Rafael David.'
He bowed again, and Judith laughed unwillingly.

'You hardly need introduction, Mr—*Señor* David?'

'I would prefer Rafael.' He leaned gracefully against

one of the flats, looking down into her face. 'My doctor
vetoed any use of my voice at all for a time, and when I
collided with you I was still under the ban. Which was
also the reason for my sinister disguise—to keep the air
from the vocal cords during my daily run.'

'I thought you were attacking me,' murmured Judith,
keeping her eyes on her wineglass.

'I was on the point of breaking my vow of silence
when *you* attacked *me*,' he said with an attractive
chuckle, and Judith glanced up to see him fingering his
chin ruefully. 'Before I could recover you ran like the
wind and I was left alone to wonder who you were.'

Unaccustomed colour rose beneath Judith's olive
skin. She felt uncomfortable; unhappily aware that they
were the centre of attention, and looked round vainly
for Honor.

'I must rejoin my sister . . .' she began, but he
forestalled her.

'Martin will be very happy to look after Mrs Gregg—
do you grudge me a few minutes of your time, Miss
Russell?'

'No, not particularly, but everyone else does,' she
said tartly. 'I'm nothing to do with the concert—you
should be with the people who are.'

Rafael regarded her with slight surprise.

'But you must surely like music, Miss Russell?'

She shook her head emphatically. 'Not very much,
I'm afraid.'

'Tell me then—if you are not a music-lover, why did
you come to the performance tonight?'

'To please Honor, my sister, as much as anything,'
said Judith candidly, and sipped a little wine to avoid
his look, now trained on her face.

He sighed. 'Then the music tonight gave you no
pleasure at all!'

'I wouldn't say that,' she answered slowly, 'but I
must be honest and admit that a large part of the
enjoyment was the sheer sense of occasion, the
excitement of knowing I was present at something out
of the ordinary.'

Rafael bent his head to look into her eyes.

'And what exactly was it that you found so extraordinary?' The note of indulgence in the celebrated voice irritated Judith.

'The mere fact that I was actually sitting there listening to classical music at all, I suppose.' She looked very squarely into the amused, translucent eyes. 'Beyond the top twenty in the pop charts I neither know nor care much about music, Mr David. I've never been to an opera before tonight, and can hardly tell Bach from the Beatles. I'm the non-musical member of my family—my mother used to say I couldn't carry a tune in a bucket.'

CHAPTER THREE

JUDITH left Rafael gazing after her, champagne bottle in hand, and went over to thank Miss Gresham and say good night. She had never felt so conspicuous in her entire life before, and her face burned as curious stares were trained on her from all sides. When she reached Honor she told her firmly she was tired and wanted to slip off early, promising her anxious sister she would ring for a taxi from the theatre foyer. Judith made her escape thankfully, and ran swiftly down the stairs to the ornate double doors of the exit, shivering a little as she left the theatre, but with no intention of wasting money on a taxi for the comparatively short distance to Chantry Lane. She set out briskly, her high black satin heels ringing on the cobbles as she picked her way across the square from the theatre and walked through the town centre before turning into the road that skirted the park. Abbey Road was long and curving, with the trees of the park lining the pavement on one side, and large, eighteenth-century houses on the other, the latter used mainly as offices by day, but dark and shuttered at this time of the morning. There were street lamps at intervals, but in between their pools of light the road was dark and deserted, the night starless and overcast.

Judith hurried along, preoccupied with her meeting with the celebrated Rafael David and his astounding apology. In one way it was very reassuring to learn the identity of her masked assailant, though she could hardly call him that, she decided, they had merely collided, to be accurate, but his disclosure had somehow been part and parcel of the entire evening. Her emotions felt battered and limp after responding to the music with such unexpected intensity. If, of course, it was solely the music that had affected her so strongly. If Mr Soames the curate had stood there with a dagger in his belt and a flower in his hand Judith had an idea her reaction would have been vastly different. In her abstraction she was never quite sure when she first heard footsteps behind her. She halted and looked behind her. The road was deserted, and she scowled, annoyed with herself. Before bumping into Rafael in the park she had never suffered from nerves in her life. She walked on doggedly, uncertain whether the noise she could hear was footsteps or the thudding of her own heart. Judith swallowed and began to hurry, almost running as she rounded the corner of Chantry Lane, which was even darker, only the light of a solitary street lamp at the far end giving any illumination; all the houses were in darkness at this hour. She paused, then went on walking slowly. *Now* she was quite sure. And angry. Within a few yards of Chantry Cottage she swung round and turned on her pursuer, who loomed large and oddly familiar, wearing a mask . . . Not again!

'This is too much,' she said furiously, peering through the darkness. 'Is this your idea of a joke——' Too late she realised her mistake. At close quarters the odour of the man was unwashed flesh and greasy wool, and the mask was a stocking pulled over his face. With a muffled scream she flung up her arm but was too late, a heavy blow crashed down on her skull and the night exploded.

Judith came to slowly, wondering why the bed was moving. She tried to sit up, but pain knifed through her head. She subsided obediently as Honor's voice scolded her and told her to lie still. But it was difficult to lie still, because the bed was bobbing about.

'Honor,' she whispered hoarsely, trying to open her eyes.

'Yes, darling, I'm here.' Honor sounded different, older. Perhaps it was someone else. Judith tried again.

'Mother? Is that you?'

'No, you were right the first time. It's Honor, but keep still. *Please!*'

Honor sounded quite desperate, so Judith did her best to comply. God, what a headache, and she felt rather sick, too, now she came to think of it.

'I'm sorry to be unoriginal,' she said apologetically, 'but where am I?'

'Nearly at the hospital,' said Honor soothingly, 'shan't be long now.'

'But it's my day off,' objected Judith feebly.

The motion stopped. Blessed relief.

'I'm in a car,' she said, pleased to solve the problem.

'Give her to me,' ordered a masculine voice, and she felt herself taken into strong arms that held her with infinite care. Judith relaxed with a sigh. The scent of this man was familiar. She was safe now.

'It *is* you this time,' she muttered. 'I know you.'

'And I know you too, *querida*.' The voice was caressing, and Judith faded into oblivion again, waking only to the blurred, but hideous reality of injections and stitches in her scalp before she was wheeled off to have an X-ray of her skull.

'Perfectly still now, Judith,' said a voice she knew.

Judith did what she was told until it was all over, then smiled at the radiotherapist groggily.

'Hi, Kevin—sorry to get you up or anything.'

The red-haired young man smiled back at her, winking.

'Hadn't gone to bed, darlin', at least, not to mine.'

'Philandering so-and-so,' said Judith amiably, and let him settle her in the wheelchair and call for the nurse.

'Will I live?' she asked.

'Let you know in a few minutes, sweetie. I'm not so sure about the staff in Casualty, though. Expiring with excitement they are out there.'

'Why?'

'Not only is Martin Gresham out there with your sister, but our operatic celebrity as well, snookums, the latter with your blood all over his frilly white shirt.'

'My *blood*?' cried Judith wildly. 'How much? What happened?'

'You were mugged, but you'll survive, a nice strong girl like you. Here's Nurse Singh. She'll take you back and put you to bye-byes.'

'What? I want to go home——'

'Save it for Sister Casualty, darlin'. If you win an argument with her you'll be in the Guinness Book of Records!'

Glumly Judith let herself be wheeled to a side-ward, where the little Indian nurse put her efficiently to bed before Sister Ames, ruling despot of Casualty, came in.

'Well, Miss Russell,' she said disapprovingly. 'A nice thing to happen, I must say. What on earth were you doing out at that time of night on your own?'

'I don't suppose you'll believe me when I tell you I was trying to get out of the public eye,' murmured Judith regretfully. 'Not very successful, was I?'

Sister chose to ignore this, and took Judith's wrist in a cool hand.

'A good night's sleep is what you need. I'll send Nurse Singh for Mrs Gregg, but she may stay for five minutes only. Good night.'

'Good night, Sister. Thank you, Sister,' said Judith automatically, then smiled apologetically as Honor's anxious face peered cautiously round the door. Honor tip-toed in as Sister Ames left, her face white and strained.

'Oh Judith,' she said huskily, and sat down by the bed, taking Judith's hand in hers. 'What on earth happened? Why did you walk home by yourself?'

'I was dead keen to get away from—from the theatre, and I didn't want to spoil your fun, so I fibbed about a taxi.' Judith smiled drowsily. 'Silly of me wasn't it?'

'Did you see who attacked you, darling? Was it the same man as before?' Honor's worried frown changed to a look of astonishment at the mischievous smile that lit Judith's face.

'No, sis, it wasn't—that I do know!' Judith laughed a little, then winced, and Honor got up to go. Judith's eyes flew open as Honor leaned down to kiss her good night. In consternation she stared at the stains on Honor's pretty cream dress. 'What on earth—is that mine?' Remembrance suddenly returned to her. 'Kevin said Rafael was covered in blood too. Have I any left, for heaven's sake?'

'The odd pint or two—don't worry. If you're very good perhaps you can come home tomorrow.'

'I'm so sorry, Honor—right in the thick of Arts Week, too. I'll try not to get in the way.' Judith patted Honor's cheek in remorse. 'By the way, don't tell Mother. Imagine her reaction if she heard I'd been attacked with the proverbial blunt instrument!'

'We'll tell her when you feel better. Good night, love.' Honor squeezed Judith's hand and turned to go.

'When you see Rafael tell him I'm sorry about his shirt,' murmured Judith, half asleep.

'I will. Go to sleep now, good night.'

Judith was allowed home next morning. Her X-ray had been normal and she was perfectly rational, so she was discharged with a warning to keep very quiet, and to take the rest of the week off. Honor was waiting with a change of clothes, and drove her back to Chantry Cottage in her old Morris Minor well before ten.

'Can I trust you to stay quietly on the sofa while I do my stint at Gresham House?' asked Honor, with an air of militance rather unusual for her. She looked tired, and Judith was consumed with guilt.

'Yes, of course, love. I'm fine, honestly. Did I cause a tremendous fuss last night?'

'You certainly did,' said Honor bluntly. 'Luckily the party broke up about half an hour after you left, everyone there being so much involved in the rest of Arts Week, and Martin felt Rafael had done more than enough anyway. The Greshams gave me a lift home and there you were, literally lying in the gutter, blood over your face, looking like a corpse.' Her face suddenly creased, and tears gathered in her eyes. 'God, Judith, it was such a ghastly shock!'

Remorsefully Judith put her arms round her sister and held her close.

'I'm terribly sorry, love, but I never dreamed of anything like that happening in staid old Hardwick.'

Honor sniffed and detached herself, wiping her eyes with a tissue, a watery smile on her face.

'You should have heard the commotion when the car stopped. Miss Gresham was the only one to keep cool; Martin was barking orders in true parade-ground manner while Rafael threw himself out of the car and wrapped his jacket round you before picking you up, swearing volubly in what I presume was Spanish, by which time most of the neighbours were either in the street or hanging out of windows to see what was causing the commotion.'

'A bit late weren't they? I could have done with more interest earlier on!'

Honor pushed Judith gently down on the sofa. Judith subsided gratefully, glad of the cushions Honor piled behind her. She had studied her reflection in the hospital mirror earlier that morning, and had felt rather depressed by it, but sensibly consoled herself with the thought that it could have been worse.

Honor brought her a tray of coffee, left books and magazines and prepared to depart.

'By the way,' asked Judith, 'did *you* take my bits and pieces of jewellery before I went into X-ray?'

Honor bit her lip. 'No, love. That's why the man mugged you, I'm afraid. He took off with your purse and all the jewellery you were wearing.'

Judith put a brave face on it until Honor left, but when she was alone she turned her face into her pillow and wept. Her gold signet ring and watch had been presents from her parents on her twenty-first birthday, and to make things worse she had been wearing the garnet pendant and earrings left to her by her grandmother. The thief was welcome to the purse and the money in it, but the other items were all of sentimental rather than intrinsic value, and irreplace-

able. Her tears lasted only a short time before she took
herself in hand. The outcome could have been much
more sinister, she told herself firmly. The trinkets were,
after all, only *things*. The man could have really beaten
her up, or worse, which would really have been
something to moan about.

Judith's peace was short-lived. Mrs Dean, from the
cottage next door, rang the bell shortly afterwards to
ask perfunctorily how she was before firing questions
about Rafael David at her, going on at length about
how thrilling it must have been to have been borne off
to hospital in his arms—almost worth being mugged
for, she laughed, and went off reluctantly when Judith
seemed unable to enjoy the joke. Mrs Dean was the first
of many. A steady stream of neighbours 'just popped
in' until Judith began to feel like a sideshow at a fair,
and was thoroughly out of sorts by the time Honor
came rushing in at noon.

'I feel like a freak at a fairground,' Judith said, trying
to laugh, but her head was aching abominably and
Honor was quick to note how heavy her sister's eyes
looked, and how pale she was beneath the tan.

'Let me get you a spot of lunch, then I must dash off
to the church—there's a piano recital there, and tonight
it's the Tudor Masque in the Court House, so I'll be
pretty well occupied today, I'm afraid. I hate leaving
you——'

'I don't want lunch, Honor, and I'll be just fine. I'll
get something for myself when I'm a bit more disposed
towards food,' said Judith firmly. 'Just forget all about
me and——'

The doorbell rang, and Honor went to answer it,
returning with an exquisite bouquet of red carnations.
Judith's eyebrows shot into her hair as she took the
card from the envelope. It said quite simply 'Rafael'.
She thrust it at Honor, and lay back, groaning.

'What's he trying to *do*, Honor? Do you mean to say
he ordered those from the florist in town? I'll be the sole
topic of conversation in Hardwick for weeks!'

'No, he didn't,' said Honor severely. 'He ordered
them from Coventry and obviously paid an arm and a

leg to have them delivered all the way over here, so don't be so ungracious.'

Judith looked a little shame-faced. 'I beg his pardon *in absentia*. It's just that I don't like all this sudden notoriety—oh my God!'

It was the doorbell again. Honor returned with a tall young constable, who removed his helmet and greeted Judith politely as he took out his notebook.

'This is P.C. Baker, Judith,' said Honor. 'My sister, Judith Russell, constable.'

'Good afternoon, Miss Russell. If I could just have a few details about your unfortunate mishap last night?'

Judith smiled as politely as she could manage, and supplied the grave young policeman with as much information as she could, which added up to very little when it was down on paper.

'Would you recognise him if you saw him again?' asked P.C. Baker.

'It was very dark, and the man had something over his face—I think it was a stocking. I have no idea what he looked like. I just had an impression of height, and the man was fairly hefty; beyond that nothing. It all happened so quickly.'

The policeman rose to leave. 'We've had one or two break-ins in the town recently. Possibly the burglar has extended his field to G.B.H.—grievous bodily harm, miss,' he added. He made a list of the jewellery taken and took his leave.

Honor saw him out and came back, shaking her head. 'They say it's a sign of age when the policemen start looking young, but that one looked barely out of school!'

'I don't think he holds out much chance of recovering the jewellery,' said Judith, sighing. 'Never mind——' she caught sight of her watch. 'You'd better get your skates on, Honor, or you'll be late.'

'Heavens, yes.' Honor gave a worried look at Judith. 'Are you sure you'll be all right? You look very washed out.'

'I'll be just fine after a rest,' said Judith firmly, 'now for goodness sake get back to your piano recital.'

Not long after Honor's departure a reporter turned up at the cottage, complete with photographer, demanding chapter and verse about Judith's attack, plus any details about Rafael David she could supply. Judith adamantly refused to let them in, or to give any details, much less allow herself to be photographed with her head wound on display, and the ensuing heated argument left her so aerated she banged the door shut in the young men's faces and collapsed on the sitting-room sofa wishing she were in Timbuctu or Tibet, or anywhere but Hardwick at that particular moment in time.

It was a quieter after that. Thoroughly worn out Judith slipped off into an uneasy doze, disturbed by vague formless dreams, waking finally to the insistent shrill of the telephone. She sat up groggily and stared balefully at the instrument on the writing desk. It went on ringing, torturing her sensitive head, and she got up to answer it merely to stop the noise. Her cautious 'hello' was answered by Miss Gresham's brisk, cheerful voice.

'Judith? Lavinia Gresham here. How are you feeling, my dear?'

'Not too bad, thank you. I'd feel better if my neighbours were less well-meaning, I'm afraid. I'm a bit of a nine-day wonder at the moment.'

Miss Gresham chuckled. 'I can imagine. Honor's just been telling me about your morning, and I gather the police have been, as well as all your visitors, which leads me to my suggestion. Why not come over here for a day or so, until you feel better.'

Judith blinked, not certain what Miss Gresham meant.

'I'm sorry,' she said blankly, 'over where?'

'To Gresham House. Plenty of peace and quiet, rooms to spare. Have a good rest before you start pummelling your patients about again.'

'That's awfully kind, but I couldn't impose. I mean you already have a guest. Besides there's Honor . . .'

'She'll come and stay too, of course. Very convenient anyway, if she's at Martin's beck and call this week.

And don't worry about our other guest. He's leaving.'
There was a discernible dry note in the kind, casual
voice.

Judith wavered, not knowing what to say, then it
occurred to her how marvellous it would be for Honor,
her mind made up as the doorbell began ringing again.
She would go mad if she stayed here.

'Well, in that case, Miss Gresham, I accept gratefully.
I *would* like a break from my sudden popularity.' The
caller had taken to banging the knocker and leaning on
the bell at the same time, and Judith was barely able to
make out something about a car calling for her in ten
minutes before she put the receiver down.

Irritably Judith threw open the door to find yet
another reporter, who was even more importunate than
the one earlier, but she gave him short shrift and got rid
of him by the simple expedient of refusing to say
anything at all before closing the door with a final click.
Angry and tired she climbed the stairs wearily to put a
few things in an overnight bag. A glimpse of her face in
her dressing-table mirror was depressing, and she
brushed her hair gingerly, wincing at the sharp spasm of
pain as she ventured too near her wound. One eyelid
was already dark with a rapidly ripening bruise, so eye
make-up seemed pointless. She touched a lipstick to her
mouth, arranged her hair as skilfully as possible to hide
the dressing, then went slowly downstairs as she heard a
car draw up outside. It was the Gresham Range Rover,
with Harry Carey, the bailiff, at the wheel. He rang the
bell and Judith picked up her bag, collected her novel to
put in it, and went to the door. Harry greeted her
sympathetically and helped her into the front seat,
winking cheerfully at her as the curtains twitched in
various windows nearby.

'Bet they wonder what you're up to next,' he said
cheerfully as he drove off.

'I'm better entertainment than Arts Week at the
moment,' answered Judith with a rueful smile. 'There
hasn't been so much excitement in Chantry Lane for
years!'

It was only a short distance to Gresham House,

which was on the outskirts of the town, its extensive grounds forming the west boundary of Abbey Park. Judith had never been inside the gardens before, and looked about her with interest as they drove along a winding carriage-way through parkland dotted with Jacobs sheep before halting on the balustraded stretch of ground in front of the Palladian façade of the house. There was a pair of stone staircases leading up to the big main portico, and Judith eyed them with a sigh. Normally she could have run up them easily with a suitcase under each arm, but today their steep ascent looked like a mountain face. While Harry was helping her alight from the car a man strolled round the corner of the great grey stone pile and came towards them. Judith stared at him in dismay.

'I thought you were leaving!' she blurted, without finesse, and Rafael David's lean-featured face looked quizzical as he strolled up to the Range Rover.

'I am. Soon.' He smiled at Harry Carey and held out his hand for Judith's bag. 'Come, Miss Russell. You look a little fragile. Let me help you up the steps.'

With a word of thanks to the bailiff Judith found herself firmly but gently assisted up the long flight of stone steps to the house.

'I can manage, really,' she protested, but the rock-hard arm stayed under her elbow until they reached the top. With embarrassment she suddenly remembered the flowers, hot at her lack of manners.

'I must thank you for the carnations, Mr David,' she said stiffly, avoiding the brilliant eyes that were examining her face with such solicitude. All her impressions of the evening before had been hazy, with Rafael David and his operatic roles all fused into some costumed, theatrical prototype, but now, in the clear light of day, this man in the casual dark blue track suit was different. Muscular and non-fictional, with no atmosphere of the theatre about him at all.

'I'm glad they pleased you,' he said gravely, and ushered her into the big, galleried hall. 'Miss Gresham apologises that she was obliged to attend the piano recital, and says you are to make yourself at home and I

am to take great care of you until she returns.' He
pulled a bell-cord at the side of the fireplace. 'Mrs
Carey, the housekeeper, will show you to your room,
then perhaps you will join me in the conservatory for a
late lunch?'

Judith thanked him formally, then turned away to
greet Mrs Carey as she appeared from the back of the
house. Here she was on familiar ground at least, as Mrs
Carey had once been one of her patients.

'Hello, Mrs C, how's the shoulder these days?' she
asked as she followed the woman up past the portraits
lining the staircase.

'Much better, Miss Russell. But how are *you*? None
too clever, by the look of you.' The woman's plump
face was sympathetic. 'Coming to something when a
decent girl can't walk the streets if she's a mind to.'

Judith concealed a grin at Mrs Carey's ambiguous
turn of phrase, and followed her into a pleasant airy
bedroom at the back of the house. It overlooked a
terrace with steps leading down to a formal rose-garden
with a little stone fountain. The distant tinkling of the
water was soothing; so was the room, its flowered
curtains and carpet much less grand than Judith had
expected. She looked longingly at the bed, plagued by a
feeling of nausea, and wanting nothing more than to lay
her throbbing head on the cool pillow and let the world
go by. She turned to Mrs Carey with a persuasive smile.

'Would you be a darling and explain to Mr David
that I can't face lunch, Mrs C, my digestive system
hasn't recovered from my adventure last night and what
I really need is a quiet couple of hours on that heavenly
bed. If he's leaving before I get up, please say goodbye
for me.'

'Yes, my dear, of course.' Mrs Carey waved to a door
in the corner. 'This is one of the rooms with a
bathroom, so you'll be nice and private. Have a good
rest and you'll feel much better, I'm sure.'

Gratefully Judith nodded, slid out of her shirt and
slacks and climbed beneath the covers with a sigh. How
quiet it was, she thought dreamily, no one would think
a busy market town was only a short distance away.

Woodpigeons were cooing somewhere near at hand, and their soporific sound was the last thing she heard as she fell deeply asleep.

Judith woke to the sound of the stable clock chiming four, and found she felt very much better as she washed and put on the fresh pink blouse and white linen skirt brought with her. As she was brushing her hair carefully into something more like its usual shining fall there was a tap on the door and Miss Gresham came in, smiling.

'You look rather better than when I saw you last, Judith.'

Judith chuckled. 'From all I hear I'd have quite a job to look worse!'

'Very true. Don't let it happen again, my dear. We were all, in our various ways, very upset.' Miss Gresham's eyes twinkled. 'Some of us more colourfully than others, I might add.'

'If you mean the amount of blood I managed to spill over everyone it's a miracle I have any left from the somewhat differing accounts I've been given!' Judith pulled a face, then remembered her manners hurriedly. 'I haven't said how grateful I am to be here, Miss Gresham. You're very kind.'

'Nonsense. No trouble at all. Now come and have some tea—Rafael tells me you've had no lunch.'

'No. For once my appetite is missing, but the thought of tea is very tempting.'

Miss Gresham preceded Judith from the room, throwing a considering look over her shoulder as they went downstairs.

'You still look a bit peaky, Judith—though possibly that eye of yours is contributing to the general effect.'

Judith searched in her bag and produced a pair of large-lensed sunglasses and slid them on. 'Better?' she asked cheerfully.

'A great improvement. Let's take a short-cut through the drawing room and join Rafael on the terrace,' said Miss Gresham.

Judith frowned. 'I thought he would have gone by now.'

Miss Gresham gave her a bland, innocent look. 'For some reason he decided to put off leaving for London until tomorrow.'

Tea was laid on a glass-topped table on the terrace, a gaily coloured umbrella shielding the tray from the sun. Rafael was leaning against the stone balustrade, deep in brooding thought near an urn full of geraniums and trailing blue lobelia. He turned sharply at the sound of footsteps, a sudden, glinting smile lighting his dark-skinned face as he came forward to greet them, his eyes reflecting the sun.

'Miss Russell—you are feeling better?'

'Much better, thank you,' answered Judith politely. 'I'm sorry I couldn't join you for lunch, I was feeling a little off-colour.'

'It is hardly surprising,' he said, his face instantly sombre. 'It is a miracle you escaped so lightly.'

So lightly! Judith looked at him with dislike. 'It's probably thanks to having such a thick skull,' she said sweetly.

'I cannot agree with you there,' he said swiftly, laughter in his eyes. 'It must have been your beautiful hair which saved you from more serious injury.'

'I'll take care not to let anything similar happen a third time,' said Judith acidly.

'A third time?' asked Miss Gresham with interest. 'Has something like this happened to you before, then Judith?'

'Yes, quite recently, but I'm trying to break myself of the habit.' Judith gave Rafael a bright, challenging look, and Miss Gresham smiled, her shrewd blue eyes watching them with enjoyment while Rafael, sudden colour in his face, explained about his first encounter with Judith in the park.

'I did not know who she was until last night,' he said. 'It was a great surprise to look up from the stage and see my mystery lady sitting there beside you, Aunt Vinnie.'

'I see,' said Miss Gresham benignly. 'Now let's enjoy some tea—Judith was just telling me her appetite had returned.'

At once Rafael installed both women at the table, offering Judith a silver plate filled with tempting sandwiches while Miss Gresham poured tea.

'I thought you were on the point of leaving,' Judith said to him as he sat beside her. 'Didn't I read somewhere that all you opera stars lead computerised lives with your programmes mapped out years ahead?'

Rafael's face went blank.

'Even the computer is at the mercy of human fallibility occasionally, Miss Russell.'

'I'm sure she won't mind if we all call her Judith,' interrupted Miss Gresham, and held out her hand for Rafael's cup. 'Let me give you some tea, dear boy.'

He drank it sugarless, and with lemon, Judith noticed idly, and wondered how he came to be in Hardwick for such a protracted spell.

'Are you on holiday, Mr David?' she asked, more in the line of keeping up a conversation than from any real interest.

'I will answer only if you call me Rafael,' he said with emphasis. 'And I am not precisely on holiday.'

'More like a spot of sick leave—which makes you two invalids together,' said Miss Gresham cheerfully.

Judith gave a surreptitious glance at the lithe, athletic figure beside her, surprised. Anything less like an invalid was hard to imagine.

'A slight fatigue of the throat,' he said, in response to her unspoken question. 'The rest of my body is as usual.'

Pretty fantastic, admitted Judith privately, thinking of him as he had been on stage the night before, but as Don José, not the unhappy Ruggiero. She checked her errant thoughts sharply, having no intention of letting herself dwell on Rafael David in any shape or form. He was a bird of passage, exotic and entirely outside a nice, normal physiotherapist's scheme of things, and would be soon winging on his way again into the frenetic round of opera-houses, hotels and airports that were the fabric of his life, the very thought of which was anathema to her.

'How did the recital go?' asked Judith hurriedly, to change the subject.

'Very well. The church was full—still lots of tourists about. Honor said she'd pick up some things on her way home. She can have the room next to yours.'

'I feel I'm being rather a nuisance over a mere knock on the head,' said Judith uncomfortably.

'You were very foolish to walk home alone,' said Rafael, his voice suddenly harsh. 'When we found you lying there for a moment I thought——'

'Yes, well it wasn't nearly as bad as it looked,' interposed Miss Gresham hastily. 'Fortunately Judith has merely learned a rather painful lesson. Ah, here comes Mrs Carey to clear away—I'll go inside with her and have a talk on the important subject of dinner. We're obliged to eat barbarously early because of this Masque thing.'

'Do you attend everything all week?' asked Judith, impressed.

'I do indeed, unless old age and sheer fatigue stop my gallop towards the latter part. And some things are repeated, of course. I don't sit through things twice.' Miss Gresham leaned forward to pat Rafael's hand. 'Unless you'd like to sing again, Rafael. I could listen to you indefinitely.'

'Thank you, Aunt Vinnie. Alas, I cannot oblige.' He raised her hand to his lips, the look in his eyes tender as he smiled at her.

'Of course not, dear boy, you've already done more than enough—no, don't get up.' With a wave of her hand she went into the house, leaving Judith and Rafael together in a silence which lengthened as the sun sank lower in the sky.

'Did you miss lunch just to avoid me?' he asked at last, his face moody.

'No,' said Judith carefully. 'I really did feel ill—a quite natural result of my adventure last night, I suppose, I'm perfectly all right now. I'm not the best invalid in the world, I confess, probably because I'm hardly ever ill.'

He turned in his chair to look at her, the thickly-lashed eyes regarding her with intensity. 'You gave me the worst fright of my life last night, Judith.'

'I didn't exactly revel in the experience myself.'

'Promise me—you will never walk alone again at night.'

Judith looked away.

'Since I met you in your fancy dress in the park I've lost my taste for running there, and now it seems even walking home has become a hazard,' she said bitterly. 'This time last week life was so uncomplicated. Now it's all changed.'

'You feel that too?' he said swiftly. He took her hand, and caught her chin in his other hand, turning her face gently towards him, his iridescent eyes holding hers. 'When I looked up and saw you in Martin's box at the theatre I almost missed a note. This is not a habit of mine, you understand. I had thought I would never see you again, and the memory of your beautiful, frightened face haunted me after that evening in the park. I was stupid—all I had to do was take off that cursed mask, but for a moment I lost my wits, I was struck dumb—me, Rafael David, with my repertoire of countless roles, could think of nothing to say!'

Judith gazed at him, eyes wide with astonishment at the sudden intensity of his voice, not sure of what he was saying. Was this some new kind of come-on—was this some particular type of technique he found successful with women? But as he leaned closer the familiar scent of him was in her nostrils, and in spite of herself her heart beat faster as she gazed silently into his eyes. She said nothing as Rafael released her chin to take the sunglasses from her gently. He stared at the bruised eyelid below the dressing on her hairline, and leaned forward until his lips touched her cheek below her eye. Judith sat motionless beneath the feather-light touch, knowing she ought to say something flippant, get up and leave, do anything other than just sit here, helpless, but she stayed where she was as his hand touched her bright hair just above the wound.

'Querida,' he said softly, 'I could kill the man who did this——' and his lips moved lower until they rested on hers. Judith's mouth quivered at the contact, and his hands grasped her shoulders fiercely, his mouth deepening its pressure, when the sound of approaching voices forced Rafael to release her. With a choked curse he moved away quickly, rising to his feet as Honor appeared round the corner of the house with Martin. In the flurry of enquiries about the invalid's health Judith managed to regain something like her normal composure, hoping the others noticed nothing amiss. She thrust the sunglasses back on her nose, glad to hide behind them, her dark eyes dazed. Rafael's kiss had startled her considerably, shaking her to the foundations, making her angry now the first shock was wearing off. What a nerve he had, now she came to think of it, making love to her the moment they were alone, as if it were his divine right, or something.

'How lucky you are to be able to dodge this Masque thing tonight,' Martin was saying ruefully. 'It must be nearly in the eighties again this afternoon, and no doubt the Court House will be packed.'

'Enough tickets have been sold for it,' agreed practical Honor, 'though I suppose we can hardly expect an evening like last night. That was unique.'

'It was to your taste, Honor?' asked Rafael, and cast a gleaming look at Judith. 'In all the ensuing drama I did not have an opportunity to ask you last night. Did you like the music, or are you like your sister—tone deaf?'

'I am *not* tone deaf,' contradicted Judith. 'Music is something I can take or leave, that's all—which didn't prevent me from enjoying the concert, just the same.'

'It was a magical evening,' said Honor warmly, 'everywhere I've been today it's been the main topic of conversation, except for Judith's horrible adventure, that is.'

'And I'm sure we don't want to discuss that any more,' said Judith quickly. 'Everyone must be bored to tears with the topic by now.'

Honor looked at her searchingly and held out her hand.

'Come on, darling, let's go upstairs and tidy up. Mrs Carey's shown me where I'm sleeping.'

'Join us here for a drink in half an hour or so,'

suggested Martin, and yawned. 'I think I'll have a cold shower.'

'I, too,' murmured Rafael, his eyes meeting Judith's. She turned away, her face hot as she followed Honor into the house.

'How are you really?' asked Honor when they were in Judith's room.

'I'm fine, honestly.' Judith stretched out on the bed with a sigh. 'Not up to a game of squash or a six mile run, but I'm not so bad. Don't worry. It's an ill wind, anyway, Honor—at least you're under the same roof as Martin for the night.'

Honor dimpled. 'True. But I'd have preferred a slightly less dramatic reason. You looked very flustered when Martin and I arrived, by the way. Had you been crossing swords with Rafael?'

'M'm. Something like that.'

'Don't you like him, Judith?'

Judith shrugged.

'You don't *like* someone like Rafael David, Honor. You admire him from the audience if you're lucky enough to see him perform. But people like him aren't part of daily life.'

'Well personally I think he's rather gorgeous.' Honor looked demure as she unpacked a dress from the suitcase brought with her.

'Do you now,' said Judith mockingly, and got up to run a bath.

Half an hour later she felt a great deal more like herself again in the jade green dress Honor had brought, her hair gleaming, her face lightly made up and the offending eye hidden behind her sunglasses. Judith eyed herself in the mirror. The dark glasses looked a bit stagey at this time of the evening, but it couldn't be helped. She slid strappy flat white sandals on her brown feet and waited for Honor, who arrived in a rush in a blue voile shirtwaister, ready for her stint at the Court House.

'How do I look?' she demanded, leaning to peer in the mirror.

'A touch more eye-shadow, and perhaps a touch of mascara,' said Judith. 'Keep still, I'll do it for you.'

Deftly she accentuated Honor's eyes a little and drew back to admire her handiwork.

'Not too much I hope.' Honor examined herself critically, then smiled, pleased. 'Makes my eyes look bigger.'

'All the better to see Martin with, Grandma. Come on, we'd better go down.'

Miss Gresham was seated at the table on the terrace, a glass of sherry in front of her, the two men leaning against the balustrade. The heat had gone from the sun, and a light evening breeze rustled in the trees. Rafael, his grey velvet trousers and white silk shirt a sharp contrast to Martin's dark, formal suit, was deep in conversation with his friend, his face dark against the glow of sunset as he waved a hand in emphasis to some point he was making. The men turned as the sisters appeared, Martin hastening to offer them drinks from the tray on the table. Judith accepted a glass of fresh orange juice with a dash of gin, and set out to be deliberately convivial, determined to dismiss any lingering aura of invalid.

'I feel an utter fraud, really,' she said, smiling ruefully at Miss Gresham. 'I'm as fit as a fiddle now.'

'I doubt you would be if you'd stayed at home,' said Miss Gresham, eyes twinkling. 'You sounded distinctly besieged when I was speaking to you on the telephone.'

'We're very happy to have you both here,' added Martin, and smiled at Honor. 'An unexpected privilege.'

'How long does this Masque of yours go on tonight, Martin?' asked Rafael casually, staring into his glass.

'With any luck it should be over by ten-thirty, I should think. I depend on you to keep Judith suitably entertained until then.'

'And how do you propose I do that?' Rafael's eyes lifted to Judith's face mockingly. 'She does not care for music, so a serenade is useless, alas.'

'You have no need to entertain me at all,' she said spiritedly. 'We can watch television, or read.'

Martin gave a sudden crack of laughter. 'That's a put-down for you, old chap. Not often a beautiful girl suggests reading a book while spending an evening with Rafael David!'

'A refreshing change for him.' Miss Gresham smiled fondly at Rafael and gave him her hand as she rose to her feet. 'I see Mrs Carey hovering. Dinner must be ready.'

Judith's appetite revived instantly when confronted by chilled gazpacho soup followed first by poached salmon in herb sauce and finally by a Grand Marnier soufflé. She enjoyed the meal all the more for the pleasure she knew Honor was experiencing just to be eating in company with Martin Gresham at his own table, and took pains to be pleasant to Rafael to ensure no jarring note spoiled anything for her. Judith had the feeling life might seem a trifle flat for both of them after all the excitement of the past day or two, her wry little smile catching Rafael's eye as they went together to see the others off after the meal. Thoughts of the episode in the garden made her uneasy as Rafael placed a hand beneath her elbow and strolled with her to the terrace.

'Let us drink our coffee outside,' he suggested. 'The evening is warm.'

'Won't the night air affect your voice?'

He shook his head. 'Not tonight. Come, let us sit and watch the moon rise.'

Quite a few women would sell their souls to hear him say that, thought Judith as she poured coffee.

'That is a very enigmatic look, Judith.' Rafael handed her a glass half-filled with brandy. She eyed it warily.

'And that's rather a large measure, surely.'

'Regard it as an elixir, a potion to relax you, to add warmth to your attitude towards me.' He sat down beside her, lounging at ease in the garden chair, and eyed her over the rim of his glass. 'And now tell me why you smiled, Judith.'

'It occurred to me that a good many women would give their eye-teeth to be in my shoes at this minute,' she said with a shrug, and took a cautious sip from her glass.

Rafael's eyes dropped to the pink-polished toenails

peeping from her sandals then returned to her face, his smile a sudden gleam against the darkness of his skin.

'Ah, but no one could fill those shoes so charmingly, Judith, nor is there any other company I would prefer.' He bent to look into her hastily averted face. 'What is it? Do you not care for compliments?'

'Of course,' said Judith lightly. She turned considering eyes on him. 'But yours sound so stylised, so practised—even well worn. Perhaps your approach is so direct because you have so little time to spare between engagements?'

Rafael made no reply. Judith waited uneasily. He appeared utterly relaxed beside her, yet she knew very well he was not, despite his pose. Beneath the indolence something dynamic radiated from him like rays from the sun, an inner energy that communicated itself to her from behind the negligent façade, reaching to some hidden source of life within herself. She blinked. Now that was really getting fanciful. The knock on the head had a lot to answer for.

'It is true that I have little time to develop new relationships,' Rafael said at last, so quietly Judith thought for a moment he was talking to himself. 'And no doubt you are prejudiced by the publicity I cannot avoid——'

'No,' said Judith quickly, 'not in the least. We don't read the tabloids and the rather staid broadsheet Honor takes goes in more for opera reviews—which I'm afraid I don't read—than juicy titbits about the opera-singers themselves.'

'So you know nothing about me at all?' He sounded amused.

'Not a lot. As I've said before, classical music just isn't my scene.'

'Then why are you so defensive towards me, Judith?'

'Am I?' She turned to look at him, thoughtfully. 'Well, I suppose because you're a celebrity and I'm just a sensible, ordinary girl with a worthy, but not terribly glamorous occupation.'

Rafael returned her look steadily.

'And you think that I can be attracted only to the

exotic beings of the world, with no time for those who follow less spectacular roads through life.'

'I don't know that I'd have put it quite like that, but yes, to be candid, I think that's right.'

He sighed and turned away. 'I was afraid of that.' He rose to his feet in one fluid movement and held out his hand. 'Come. Let us walk in Martin's tranquil gardens, and you shall tell me the story of your life.'

'*My* life?' Judith laughed spontaneously as she strolled with him down the shallow stone steps of the terrace to the rose garden and the tree-lined avenue beyond. 'Very dull, I'm afraid. I'm a qualified physiotherapist, I work in the hospital here in Hardwick, I live with Honor and my parents have retired to a place near Abergavenny. I like swimming, running—and walking—I play squash, badminton and I have a regular escort in the shape of a doctor from one of the medical practices in the town.'

Rafael turned towards her, frowning.

'He is your fiancé?'

'No. Marriage doesn't figure in my immediate plans.'

'Then he is your lover?'

She halted, looking at him coldly.

'That, I think, is entirely my own affair.'

'*Lo siento*—I apologise.' He gave her an odd, stiff little bow and they resumed their stroll.

By this time the moon was a sliver-thin arc of silver in the dusk, with dilatory stars making their appearance here and there to join it. It was very peaceful, only the occasional distant rumble of traffic to remind them how close they were to civilisation. Judith breathed in the scent of newly-mown grass, rising heady and green as they paced slowly along the shadowy tree-lined walk towards a gazebo, which loomed ghost-like and pale agains the sky as they approached.

'Now you know everything about me——' began Judith.

'Everything?' said Rafael quizzically.

'All the salient points, then.' Judith looked dubiously at the gazebo's shadowy interior as Rafael gestured to her to enter. It was a fanciful, rococo little construction, frivolous as a piece of scenery from an operetta.

'There is a cushioned seat inside,' Rafael said, the glint in his eyes plainly visible even in the dim light. 'Come—let us rest a little, we two poor invalids, and cherish our infirmities together for a while.'

To her disgust Judith actually *was* glad to subside on what proved to be a love-seat, cushioned in worn velvet. She sat down gratefully, not realising how close it brought Rafael until he sat down on the other half of the seat. Although they now faced in opposite directions their faces were a shade too close for comfort, and Judith kept her eyes on her feet, fairly sure Rafael's were fixed on her face in amusement.

'Right,' she said briskly. 'It's your turn. Tell me about your life.'

CHAPTER FOUR

'BUT I have lived so much longer than you, Judith. It would weary you to hear about a life devoted to nothing but the music you find so uninteresting.' He touched her cheek for an instant.

'No, it won't,' she insisted. 'I'd like to hear the authorised version instead of the gossip columnists'. Start by telling me how on earth you came to have a Welsh father.'

'He was the only son of a Welsh colliery owner. His mother died at his birth and he was a lonely child who gew up hating coal and everything to do with it. His only wish in life was to paint. My grandfather, in true patriarchal style, told him to forget such effeminate nonsense, to do a man's job in the mine, or leave home. So my father left home and made for Paris, of course, but eventually ended up in Spain. He became quite successful there and sold well, both landscapes and the occasional portrait. Then one day he was commissioned to paint the portrait of a young opera singer, fresh from her success as Carmen—and so Gwyn David met Carmelita Valentin and that was that, the overwhelming love at first sight no one believes in but everyone desires.'

'How very romantic!' Judith was fascinated. 'Go on—did they marry at once?'

'Oh yes. My mother's family did not care for the match, you understand, but she was determined. A mere six months later my father was drowned, trying to rescue his easel, which had blown from the rocks into the sea. My mother returned to her family at the Casa de las Flores in Granada, where I made my first appearance three months later, and shortly after that Carmelita Valentin returned to the operatic stage. As far as I know she never looked at another man again.'

'How sad!' Judith was deeply affected by Rafael's story. 'But I see now why you come over as all Spaniard.'

Rafael laughed. 'I hesitate to contradict, Judith, but although I never knew him, or any of his family, I resemble my Welsh father much more than my red-haired Spanish mother. Even my aptitude for music could be a joint legacy—the Welsh are a musical race.'

'So tell me more about *you*,' persisted Judith.

He shrugged. 'If you wish.'

His factual, rather matter-of-fact account of his early life failed to minimise his spectacular success in the operatic world, a hectic, exhausting saga of airflights, performances, television, recordings, endless interviews.

'You seem to have precious little time to yourself,' said Judith, awe-struck. 'Have you never wanted to marry, Rafael?'

'I did,' he said quietly. Judith's lip caught in her teeth, and she sat straighter in her seat.

'Oh,' she said blankly. 'I didn't know—forgive me.'

'How could you know? You would have been a mere child at the time. I was not so very old myself—neither was Lucia. I was just starting to make a name for myself, though only in *comprimario*—minor—roles, but beginning to be heard, and noticed. Lucia was the daughter of Claudio Matteo, the conductor. I was twenty-one and she was a year younger.' Rafael's voice hardened. 'She was very beautiful, white skin and huge eyes, the very quintessence of innocence and purity. I worshipped her. And when she told me she was expecting a child very soon after our marriage, I was ecstatic. Unhappily the father of the child was not myself, as I fondly imagined, but one of the leading tenors of the time. He was already married, unfortunately, with a string of legitimate children already to his credit. I was the poor ignorant dupe chosen as a cover of respectability.' The scorn in his voice raised the hairs on the back of Judith's neck.

'What happened?' she whispered.

'Once our marriage was—established, shall we say,' he said harshly, 'Lucia saw no need to keep up the pretence. My touch was not welcome after the caresses of the great star, so she confessed the truth to me. After which, of course, she had no cause for concern. I would not have touched her had she gone on her knees.'

'And the child?'

'It was born prematurely. Lucia died trying to give birth.' Rafael breathed in deeply. 'The day after her funeral I sang Cassio in a production of *Otello* which starred her lover in the title role. I sang well. So well I was offered the role of Cavaradossi in a forthcoming production of *Tosca*, and never sang a minor role again.'

Judith leaned towards him diffidently, and touched his cheek in turn.

'I'm so sorry, Rafael—I never dreamed, I mean I wouldn't have asked if I'd known.' She heard his sharp intake of · breath and drew back, uncertain of his reaction.

'Very few people know—or remember if they do. I'm glad you know.' His voice softened, the deadness in his tone vanished. 'All the statistics show that Rafael David married Lucia Matteo, and shortly afterwards she died tragically young in childbirth. She always swore that her father knew nothing of the affair with—with her lover, and I believed her. He was a fine man.'

'Have you never wanted to marry anyone else?' asked Judith curiously.

'No.' He gave a short laugh. 'The world is full of beautiful women, *querida*, I am not—neglected.'

'No.' Judith got up, regretting her sympathy, then wavered slightly, suddenly conscious of the throbbing in her head. Rafael sprang up to steady her.

'What is it?' he demanded. 'Are you not well?'

'Just giddy for a moment—I must have got up too suddenly.'

Without warning he gathered her into his arms, holding her close. 'Oh Judith,' he groaned, 'I feel it was all my fault. You left the party to escape from me, no?'

'No! I just went home on my own much too late at night, got coshed for my pains and will never, ever do it again.' A little laugh shook her as she leaned against Rafael's warm, hard body. 'I knew it was you before you spoke to me at the party.'

He chuckled softly.

'You mean you saw my name on the programme!'

'No, idiot—I meant your smell——'

'*Dios!*'

'No, no, your scent, then, if you want a more graceful word. When we fell in a heap together on that memorable occasion in the park would you believe that one tiny brain cell wasn't panicking madly like the rest. It was making a note of your particular, personal fragrance, to use a better word. It was the same last night when you leaned alongside me on the stage.' Judith gave a little breathless laugh and sniffed delicately. 'And tonight, Rafael.'

Her face was jerked up to his by a peremptory finger.

'Do you know what you invite by saying such things, Judith?'

A tremor ran through her. 'There was no provocation intended, I was just——'

'I know you meant none of it,' he said, suddenly fierce, 'you were teasing, little fool.' And he kissed her hard.

Judith clutched him for support, gasping in surprise, and at once his mouth softened and his arms slid round her, holding her so close his velvet-clad knee slid between hers to maintain balance, demonstrating unmistakably the effect her words had made on him. The blood beat in her cheeks at the intimacy of the contact, and she pushed at him, but Rafael only lifted his head a little and said unevenly,

'I too like to run and swim and play games, my little Amazon, but I'm bigger than you, tougher too, so I'll choose the game I enjoy best—the one only two can play.' And to emphasize his point he bent his head and took possession of her lips once more.

To feel utterly helpless was a new experience for Judith. Not that it dominated her entirely—she was too taken up with the effects of this demanding mouth, which was calling up a response from some hitherto undiscovered region deep inside her, a deep well of sensation never tapped until now. Oblivious to everything else in the world for the moment she gave herself up without reserve to the flood of heat penetrating to every part of her, unfolding to his urgency like a flower opening to the sun. She frankly adored what he was doing, revelled in his insistence, and when one of his hands moved by instinct to her breasts she arched her back, offering them proudly to his caressing fingers until the sensations they triggered off took her breath away and she tore her mouth from his to moan faintly, 'Rafael, please——'

His only answer was a rasping sound deep in his throat as his mouth searched blindly for hers again, and he crushed her cruelly tight against him. Judith flung up her arms to lock her hands behind his head, opening her mouth to his tongue, her heart thudding, her breath mingling with his in great gasps that shook them both. Without a word Rafael dropped one arm behind her knees and lifted her, striding from the gazebo deep into the cover of the beeches lining the dark, grassy avenue. He laid her urgently on the grass and flung himself down beside her, recoiling in sudden horror at Judith's cry of anguish as her head made rough contact with the hard, dry earth.

'Querida—what—Gran Dios!' Rafael hit his forehead

with the heel of his hand and helped Judith to a sitting position with care, supporting her against his shoulder. 'Your head,' he said hoarsely, 'have I injured you further? Speak, Judith—speak!'

'I will,' she said, breathless. 'Just give me a moment. I'm—I'm all right, honestly. I—I forgot I had a wound, for a moment there.'

He rubbed a hand across his eyes. 'I did not think—I am an imbecile. Forgive me, Judith.'

'It wasn't entirely your fault,' she said with justice. 'It's just that I'd never had first-hand experience before of what's meant by "the world well-lost for love". Only I rather fancy I mean "lust", don't you?'

'Do you, Judith?' he asked soberly. 'Is that what you felt? Lust?'

'Not having felt quite like that before I'm not really in a position to judge.' Judith sat erect gingerly, glad of Rafael's arm in support.

'What do you mean? You have made love before, no?'

'No—yes, well, not quite to that degree of sheer dementia, anyway,' she said candidly. 'Perhaps I could get up now——'

'Stay where you are for a moment,' he said sternly. 'I behaved—I am not sure how I behaved, but I had no right to go wild like that, at least not under these circumstances, when you are injured.'

'Then it's quite admissible with partners who are all in one piece?' she asked innocently.

'You are teasing again, *chica*,' he warned. 'This doctor of yours—do you subject him to the same treatment?'

Judith sobered. 'As I've said before, I don't consider that particular subject one for discussion. Please help me up now. It must be getting late.'

Rafael helped her to her feet, then took her arm as they walked slowly back to the house.

'Are you truly all right, Judith?' he asked with concern.

'It depends on what you mean by "all right",' she said lightly. 'I'm fully recovered from the effects of last night, I think. Now all I have to do is recover from those of tonight.'

'Which makes me feel like an animal,' he said bleakly.

'Oh please—don't. I'm not blaming you in the slightest. It was just as you said.' Judith paused as they reached the terrace, smiling at him in the soft light coming from the house. 'One of those games only two can play. We perhaps brought rather more enthusiasm to it than was wise, that's all.'

Rafael stared down at her, looking baffled, his brows meeting above his eyes. 'You perplex me, Judith. Do you take nothing seriously?'

'Of course,' she said cheerfully. 'But only when necessary. During working hours I'm a very earnest lady, I assure you. But you're not part of every day life, Rafael, are you? So let's keep it light.'

She went ahead of him into the drawing-room as the stable clock began to chime ten, catching sight of herself in one of the twin gilt-framed mirrors either side of the Adam fireplace. Her eyes were like flames in her flushed face, the discoloured one giving her a distinctly disreputable air, and her hair was a disaster. A quick, dismayed inspection of her dress did nothing to cheer her up, either. The thin green cotton was creased and crushed beyond repair. If Honor set eyes on her in this state there'd be blood on the moon, as their mother was always saying. Regretfully she turned away from the mirror to the man watching her.

'Rafael, I think it best I turn in before the others get back.'

He stood studying her, his eyes almost hidden by the thick lashes framing them. 'You mean my company palls?'

This was a long, long way from the truth, Judith realised uneasily.

'No,' she said steadily. 'I mean that if my sister sees me looking like this I'll never find an explanation to satisfy her. I can hardly change my clothes at this time of night, so I suppose I'd better just go to bed.'

Rafael's eyes dropped slightly, and she flushed as she

followed their gaze. To her embarrassment she found her dress was torn at one corner of the low, square neckline.

He gave an eloquent, despairing shrug.

'Again I apologise——'

'Please don't,' Judith said quickly. 'Good night.'

'I shall see you to your room,' he said formally, and in silence escorted her up the stairs. He opened the door of the bedroom, then stood looking at her gravely for a moment. 'I go to London tomorrow, Judith, after which I am due in Bregenz, then Verona.'

'You'll be very busy.' She looked away.

'I shall think of you.' The vibrant voice was almost inaudible.

'And I of you.' Which was an understatement.

With a stifled sound he caught her by the shoulders and kissed her roughly, opening her mouth with his before he released her to walk away without a backward glance. Judith watched him go, a hand to her mouth, then went into the bedroom and closed the door behind her, leaning on it for a moment, dazed. After a while she took off her dress and folded it into her bag out of sight, then had a hasty bath and brushed her hair, her head throbbing dully, her face still on fire. She was lying in bed, her novel open at the same unread page when Honor came in half an hour later, her face anxious.

'Feeling rough, Judith? You look very hot.' She went out of the room and came back in with a thermometer, popping it in Judith's mouth before she could protest, then inspected the dressing on her scalp, clucking her tongue when she found the patient's temperature was indeed up a couple of degrees.

'Don't worry. I'll survive.' Judith smiled at her, eyes brilliant with suppressed guilt. 'Go back down to the others. I'll be fine.'

'Did you manage to pass the evening pleasantly?' asked Honor when she was ready to leave.

'Yes. Very pleasantly.'

'You must have overdone things a bit. We'll get the

doctor in the morning if you still feel rotten.' Honor smiled lovingly and closed the door.

Judith let out an explosive sigh. She felt like a criminal. It was underhand to worry Honor unnecessarily like that when there was nothing medically wrong with her at all beyond three stitches in her scalp. The only thing that moderated Judith's guilt a little was the thought that if Honor knew the real reason for her sister's fever she would worry twice as much—at least.

Flat on her back, Judith stared at the ceiling, making herself lie still and quiet. It was difficult. Her whole body felt riotously alive. She ran her hand slowly over the curve of her shoulder, trying to imagine how it had felt to Rafael, wondering if he had liked the feel of her—a sharp stab of reminiscent sensation shot through her at the mere thought of his seeking hands, and with a groan she turned on her stomach and buried her face in her pillow. She had always wondered idly why she remained so detached during any lovemaking demanded by various men-friends. The girls who trained with her had all seemed to revel in the pastime with partners many and various, comparing skills and thrills afterwards with gusto. Judith had avoided these discussions, not caring to admit that the warmest adjective for any of her romantic passages was pleasant. At least up to now. Tonight she had learned a very surprising lesson. Everyone possessed the necessary switch, apparently. It just needed the right person to turn it on. Even if the right person turned out to be the wrong one in every possible way. And Rafael David was about as wrong as it was possible to be for someone like Judith Russell. She sighed gloomily as she thought of returning to work. It was likely to be a test of stamina. She could just picture the barrage of questions from her colleagues about her dramatic arrival in Casualty. At least tonight's episode was unknown to anyone. It was so different for Rafael, probably the type of thing he was used to, though presumably with less battered partners he was unlikely to be left frustrated, and possibly sleepless. Like she was herself.

Next morning Judith was up early, with the idea of returning to Chantry Cottage as soon as she could. Her belongings packed, the room tidy, she went quietly downstairs, the scent of tempting coffee leading her towards the morning room, a small, pleasant little apartment overlooking the terrace. Martin was alone at the breakfast table, reading the morning paper. His thin, clever face lit with a surprised smile as he got to his feet.

'Judith! Should you be up and about? Honor said you weren't too good last night.'

There was no sign of Rafael. Judith relaxed a little and sat down in the chair Martin was holding out for her.

'Good morning,' she said cheerfully, and shook out her napkin. 'I'm much better, and I really can't trespass on your hospitality any longer; it would be sheer malingering if I did.'

'I don't agree, but I think I'll leave the arguing to Honor,' he said. 'At least let me ring for something cooked, Judith—what would you like?'

'Nothing like that, thanks. Both of us are toast and coffee lovers in the morning. Honor sometimes even dodges that if I don't make a fuss.' Judith helped herself to toast and butter, and poured coffee for them both. Martin thanked her, frowning.

'She's too thin. Does she look after herself properly, Judith?'

Judith forbore to mention that apart from a disinclination for breakfast Honor enjoyed the rest of her meals as much as anyone else.

'I think she's better now I'm living with her,' she said evasively. 'Cooking for one isn't much fun, I suppose.'

'No.' Martin looked thoughtful. Judith glanced at his discarded paper and wondered if he might prefer to return to the day's news.

'Please carry on reading your paper,' she said casually. 'I shan't mind in the least.'

'I wouldn't dream of it,' he said instantly, and with a charming sincerity that made it easy to understand Honor's feelings towards him. 'It's rare I have any company at all at the breakfast table, let alone such decorative company as you, Judith. Aunt Lavinia breakfasts in her room later, but I'm a compulsive early riser, I'm afraid—legacy of my army years. It was an even earlier start this morning, as Raf needed a lift to Coventry to catch the early train.'

Judith felt a sudden flatness, the glow gone from the beautiful, sunlit morning.

'I hadn't realised he was leaving so early.' She took another piece of toast from the silver rack Martin offered, then looked at it blankly, wondering what to do with it.

'He had to be in Harley Street this morning,' said Martin. 'Check-up on his throat. I feel guilty, actually. I'm sure he should never have sung over the weekend. He was supposed to be here for a rest, not an impromptu performance.'

'I'm sure he was glad to be of help,' Judith assured him. 'It was certainly an evening Hardwick won't forget in a hurry.' Nor would she, if it came to that. In fact, it seemed Rafael was determined she would remember.

When Judith arrived home later that morning there was another delivery from the florist. This time it was a single carnation in a long white box. Judith stood in the hall, staring at the flower for a very long time before putting it in the vase with the others, then went outside to lie on the patio in the shade and daydream, reliving the previous evening over and over again, secure in the knowledge that Rafael would ring later, or if not there would be a letter from him in the morning. There was no 'phone call, however, and the feeling of enchantment faded a little overnight, only to be revived instantly when another solitary carnation arrived, anonymous but highly gratifying in the romantic message Judith assumed it was meant to convey. Honor teased gently, but grew concerned as the week wore on with nothing more tangible in the way of communication from Rafael than the daily floral delivery. Secretly Judith ran the gamut of every emotion from anger to despair as no letter arrived and the only 'phone calls were for Honor apart from a stilted enquiry from Rob about her injury.

She made a hundred excuses for Rafael's silence—he was busy, he didn't know her number, perhaps he was forbidden to speak, but deep in her heart she was anguished. Flowers were all very well, but they were not what she wanted. She wanted to hear Rafael's voice, badly needing reassurance that their brief time together had been more than just a pleasant interlude. After a few days Judith was ready to hurl the daily carnation back at the cheery girl from the florist, almost frantic with inactivity, and bitterly certain she was all kinds of fool for being dazzled by the synthetic glitter of a star obviously merely out to amuse himself for a little while with the local talent. One way and another Judith was not the most restful of company and by the weekend Honor had had enough.

'Borrow my Morris and go down to Abergavenny for the weekend,' she suggested, worried by the dark shadows under her sister's eyes.

It was a brainwave. Suddenly desperate to be free of Hardwick and all its associations Judith hugged Honor in gratitude and headed for her parents' home, determined to pull herself together and forget that she'd ever heard of Rafael David, let alone come into contact with him.

For most of the weekend she succeeded fairly well. Her mother and father were delighted to see their child, and after a few awkward explanations about her mishap had been cleared out of the way Judith was able to relax and allow herself to be spoiled a little, almost managing to put Rafael from her mind altogether during the day. But in bed alone in the dark his face was there before her eyes, vivid and ineradicable until sleep blotted out his features.

CHAPTER FIVE

ON the Sunday morning the three of them lingered late over breakfast, the table littered with newspapers, as

was usual in the Russell household. Judith was deep in
an account of a day in the life of one of her favourite
novelists when her mother emerged from her perusal of
the music and book-reviews, her eyes wide.

'What is it, Kate?' asked her husband.

'It says here that Rafael David was admitted to a
London clinic for an operation earlier on this week. Did
you know, Judith?'

Judith stared at her mother in disbelief, then shook
her head numbly.

'No. I knew he was going to a specialist in London
on Tuesday, but Martin never said a word about any
operation.' She held out a peremptory hand for the
paper. 'Let me see, please.'

The news item was brief. As Mrs Russell said, it
stated that Rafael David, the celebrated singer, had
undergone an operation in a London clinic, but gave no
details, nor any bulletin on his state of health.

'Did he seem ill, Judith?'

Far from it. Vitality had seemed to radiate from him.

'No. He was consulting an E.N.T. man about his
throat, and that's all I know.'

Kate Russell looked at her daughter's face thoughtfully
and got up to refill the coffeepot. Judith was obviously
shattered by the news item, but too wise to question her
on what was plainly a very sensitive subject her mother
merely supplied her with strong coffee and exchanged a
speaking look with her husband over their daughter's
bright head. Judith seemed unable to tear her eyes from
the stark statement, and it was some time before she
lifted her head to ask if she might ring Honor.

'Of course, darling,' said her mother matter-of-factly.
'We'll have a word when you've finished.'

Honor's number rang for such a long time Judith was
on the point of putting the 'phone down when her
sister's breathless voice finally answered.

'Sorry, Judith. I was in the bath. I had a bit of a lie-in
this morning.'

'Honor—it says in the paper that Rafael's had an
operation.'

There was a pause. 'Yes, darling,' said Honor at last.

'The specialist had the result of some tests when Rafael went down on Wednesday, and an operation was necessary. A—a small growth, I understand.'

'A growth!' Judith gripped the 'phone hard. 'What sort of growth, Honor?'

'I don't know, darling. Martin went down to see him this morning. He left very early, but I shan't expect him back until this evening. Perhaps he'll know more by then.'

Judith handed the receiver over to her mother and went upstairs. The word 'growth' turned her cold, however much she told herself it could be benign. She shivered at the possibility of malignancy. Not Rafael—not that wonderful voice silenced, surely. Life could never be so cruel. But life in a hospital had taught Judith only too thoroughly that it could. She packed her case swiftly and went down to her parents, her jacket over her arm.

'I won't stay for lunch, Mother,' she said. 'I'd sooner get back early. It's my first day back at the hospital tomorrow, so I'd better not leave it too late.'

Kate Russell had prepared a big lunch, and opened her mouth to protest, then thought better of it at a warning look from her husband.

'All right, darling.' She reached up to kiss Judith's cheek. 'Don't upset yourself too much, Judith. A growth could mean anything.' She hesitated delicately. 'I didn't think you knew him very well.'

'Neither did I,' said Judith obscurely, and kissed her father. 'Bye, Dad. I'll ring when I get home.'

'Take care, Judith,' he said soberly. 'Keep your mind on your driving. I'll just check the oil and water for you.' He went outside, leaving Judith alone with her mother.

'Are you in love with the man?' asked Kate gently.

'I've only met him a couple of times, Mother.' Judith looked away, a faint colour along her cheekbones.

'I don't think that has a lot to do with it, really, love.' Kate squeezed her hand tenderly. 'Don't get hurt, Judith.'

'Tell me how to avoid it, Mum and I will!' Judith

smiled ruefully and picked up her bag as her father
came in.

The Russells stood waving the elderly Morris out of
sight, their faces troubled.

'I just wish the poor man wasn't an opera singer,'
said Kate with a sigh as they went arm in arm into the
house.

'Why, darling?'

'Operas never have happy endings!'

The journey back to Hardwick was long. Judith forced
herself to keep her mind on the road ahead, doing her
utmost not to think of Rafael's splendid body prostrate
on a hospital bed. It was no use telling herself she was
being fanciful, that there was no earthly reason for him
to be prostrate after a throat operation; she kept
picturing him lying silent and tragic. And alone. Which
was really far-fetched—visitors were probably three
deep round his bed. Her own presence would be an
embarrassment to him rather than a comfort she told
herself savagely, and pushed the poor Morris to its limit
in an effort to get back to Hardwick as soon as
possible. It was a great relief to garage the car in the
stables at last, and with a sigh Judith set off down
Chantry Lane, pleased when Honor had the door of the
cottage open before Judith could put her key in the
lock, hugging her as she took her case.

'Welcome back; I missed you. Had a good journey?
Want some tea?'

'Yes, please.' Judith returned the hug and said
bluntly, 'Well? What news of Rafael?'

'Good news! The growth was benign, the operation a
success, and in a few days he's coming back here again
to convalesce at Gresham House, only that's strictly
secret.' Honor beamed.

Judith flopped down on the sofa, limp with relief.
'Thank God for that.'

Honor brought in a tray and sat down to pour out.
She gave Judith a very straight look. 'You sounded
absolutely flattened when you rang.'

'Not so surprising. Reading about it in cold blood in

a newspaper was a bit stark.' Judith drank her tea, avoiding Honor's eye.

'Rafael didn't want anyone to know, but it must have leaked out somehow. Martin didn't dare let on that the Press had the information.'

Judith was unprepared for the terrible feeling of hurt she experienced at her exclusion from Rafael's confidence, and answered quickly before Honor suspected how she felt.

"I do hope he gets better quickly anyway—such a rotten thing for a singer to have wrong with him.' She smiled brightly and changed the subject. 'The parents send their love; they look very well. Oh, I forgot, Honor. Dad filled the boot with plums and runner beans, tomatoes, all sorts of things from the garden. I'll pop back to the coach house in a minute and collect them.'

'That's handy,' said Honor, sudden colour in her cheeks. 'Miss Gresham's gone down to a friend in Wiltshire for a few days, so I invited Martin to dinner tonight.'

Judith's fatigue vanished. She sat up, grinning.

'Here? Well, well, who's a bold hussy, then. What brought that on, may I ask?'

'Sheer impulse before you came,' said Honor airily. 'He came straight here on his way back from London, and looked very worn. He's so fond of Rafael—and coming on top of Arts Week like this it's rather knocked him for six, I think. I felt sorry for him, so I asked him round.'

'I'm sure he jumped at it,' declared Judith with a grin.

'He seemed pleased,' agreed Honor guardedly. 'Anyway I had rather a nice joint of beef ready to cook when you got back and if Dad's sent some home-grown vegetables as a bonus we should be able to compete with Gresham House cuisine.'

'Any day! I'll just ring the parents then you can come and help me lug home the spoils. By the way,' added Judith casually, 'are the carnations still arriving?'

'Not today. It's Sunday. But there were two yesterday.'

Judith took great care to conceal the pleasure that this news gave her as she went over to the telephone to inform her parents she was back in one piece.

Later that evening she helped Honor move their small dining table near the window overlooking the back patio, and brought out Honor's wedding-present china and lit yellow candles to match the fringed linen napkins. Martin obviously appreciated the effect when Honor let him in.

'What a welcoming sight,' he said, smiling with pleasure, 'not to mention the most marvellous smell! I walked over, so I warn you I'm quite hungry. It's very kind of you to take so much trouble,' he added, turning to Honor.

'We're happy to return your hospitality,' she said, smiling back, 'what will you drink?'

Judith tactfully left them together and went off to make the gravy and strain the vegetables, enveloped in a plastic apron to protect her white shirt and trousers. They had decided against a first course, and as soon as the Yorkshire puddings were out of the oven she popped in the plum crumble to warm through and carried the main course in.

Martin plainly enjoyed the meal enormously, accepting second helpings of everything. Inevitably the conversation turned to Rafael while they ate, Judith reluctant to show too much interest, but Honor quite openly anxious to know how he was.

'It's not easy to tell' Martin looked worried. 'He's not allowed to speak yet, which doesn't exactly make for easy communication. His London agent Robin Mellor, and his wife Holly, are in strong support, but otherwise he isn't seeing anyone except me.'

'But doesn't he have relations in Spain?' asked Honor.

'No one really close. His mother was an only child, and so was he, and his father's family are completely unknown to him. He keeps up the family house in Granada, but his relatives there are all getting on a bit, and apart from a flying visit when he's in Granada he doesn't see them that often.' Martin frowned. 'Rafael's friends are too numerous to count, of course, in most countries in the world, but at this particular moment he doesn't seem to want to see anyone at all, apart from the Mellors and me.'

'Well, it must be a bit of a drag to be sociable if you can't talk,' said Judith reasonably.

'Yes, I suppose so, but it's more than that,' said Martin slowly. 'He seems so low in spirit—utterly unlike himself. Rafael and I have been friends for a long time and I've never seen him like this before. Normally he's a tower of strength, particularly in times of crisis. I mean, the time my marriage ended in divorce Raf managed to sandwich a flying visit up here between engagements, which actually meant a return trip from New York to London and back again. His sheer vitality was like a shot in the arm; exactly the thing I needed most at the time. That's why it's so disturbing to see him the way he is now, so—so switched off, somehow.'

Honor went very quiet at the mention of Martin's divorce, and began to clear away their plates. Judith helped her, giving Martin a reassuring smile.

'Operations affect people in diverse ways, you know. Sometimes the post-op blues are a bit hard to throw off.'

'Yes, of course, but as Honor knows already, I'm the world's greatest pessimist!' Martin grinned apologetically as they moved to the other end of the room to drink coffee.

Judith remained only a short while before excusing herself to do the washing up, refusing all offers of assistance. 'Fair's fair,' she said firmly. 'Honor cooked the meal, so I'll do the clearing up.' She closed the sitting room door on them and switched on the transistor in the kitchen, whistling tunelessly to it while she worked, with the aim of giving Honor and Martin as much privacy as possible.

Afterwards Judith spent a token half hour with the other two, then went to bed, pleading fatigue and the need for an early night before returning to work next day. The fatigue was genuine enough, nevertheless sleep was a long time coming as she thought of Rafael.

Martin's account of his state of mind was disturbing, and it harrowed her to think of someone vital like Rafael mute in his own self-imposed isolation in the hospital. One ray of light in her gloom was the fact that Martin stayed quite late, which seemed a step in the right direction as far as his growing friendship with Honor was concerned.

Sometimes the event dreaded in advance turns out better than expected, but for Judith her return to work was far, far worse. The other physiotherapists, nurses, cleaners, housemen, porters—it seemed everyone she spoke to all that first day had something to say about her nasty experience, not to mention her incredible luck at being borne into Casualty in Rafael David's arms. Although, to her intense relief no one seemed to have read the item on Rafael's own admission to hospital.

Her nerves stretched to breaking point Judith was thankful to arrive home at the end of a very imperfect day, only to find that no carnation had arrived for her. It was the final straw. Fighting with the urge to break down and howl she forced herself to face facts. It *had* been just a romantic little interlude, then. Something to pass the time. So now she would have to think of something absorbing to pass her own time, of which a great deal seemed to stretch out in front of her like a desert. There was no Rob now—not that she wanted him. All she wanted was Rafael, and there was no point in lying to herself. What a moron she'd been, fondly imagining an international star like Rafael David could spare more than a fleeting thought for a provincial nobody like Judith Russell.

Wisely Honor made no reference to the missing flower, nor to Judith's day, drawing her own conclusions from her sister's weary face. She served up an appetising cottage pie made from the previous day's left-over beef and let Judith come round in her own good time.

'Sorry, Honor,' said Judith eventually, after good food and a rest had smoothed her jagged edges a little. 'I'm a pig. I admit it. But it was a pig of a day, as I expected. Worse than I expected to be precise. One word about my little adventure tomorrow and I'll blow my top.'

'How's your head? Stand up to all the hard work without pain?' asked Honor with sympathy.

'M'm, so-so. Throbbing a bit, but not from the physical effort; more from the endless stream of questions about the celebrated Rafael. *Not* my harrowing experience, you note!' Judith jumped up restlessly. 'Do you mind if I dodge the washing up, love? I need some air—I'm going for a run.'

'Oh Judith, please be careful!'

'I won't go near the park, I promise. Just a leisurely jog through town.'

Judith kept her promise, not only to please Honor, but because she was sadly out of practice. The wound on her head, though healed, throbbed after only a short distance at even a moderate pace, and she went back home feeling more out of sorts than ever, and decided to take a bath.

While she was rinsing the conditioner from her hair she heard the telephone. To her surprise Honor was still on the 'phone ten minutes later. Eyebrows raised Judith made coffee and carried the mugs into the other room just as Honor was saying goodbye.

'Martin,' said Honor, her cheeks rather pink.

Judith's eyes sparkled. 'Getting rather thick, you two!'

'He was reporting on the latest news of Rafael—not from the hospital. He'd heard from Robin Mellor, Rafael's agent.'

Judith sat down, her eyes questioning. 'How is he?'

'Pretty much the same, apparently. He's very concerned.'

'Do you think Rafael knows something he's not letting on, Honor?'

'That's exactly what Martin's afraid of.' Honor bit her lip. 'And apparently Rafael's not coming here to convalesce, after all.'

Judith felt sick with disappointment, and it showed.

'Oh,' she said blankly. 'That's—that's rather a change of plan, then.'

'It seems he needs to get away by himself for a bit, apparently. His engagements have been cancelled for a month anyway, so he's going to take a holiday, according to Mr Mellor.'

'Where?' asked Judith involuntarily.

'Martin doesn't know.'

'Spain, would you say?'

Honor shook her head. 'Too well known there. Gets mobbed everywhere he goes.'

'Well it's not really any business of ours,' said Judith dully. 'We hardly know him.'

'Forgive me, Judith, but I felt you got to know him a little better than you let on, however much you make noises to the contrary.' Honor's eyes were steady. 'Did you perhaps fall in love with him just a little bit?'

Judith turned away restlessly.

'In just a day or two? Come off it, Honor. You've been reading too many romances.'

Honor looked unconvinced.

'Those carnations were fairly romantic, wouldn't you say?'

'Absurd, you mean.' Judith shook her hair free and began combing through the damp strands, covering her face.

'Are you defensive because he's famous—a celebrity, Judith?' asked Honor curiously. 'Why are you so hell-bent on refusing to admit any attraction to him?'

Judith was still for a moment, then she threw back her hair and met Honor's eyes, her face flushed and her eyes stormy.

'All right. I do admit it. When he sang that thing from *Carmen* the hair stood up on the back of my neck—not because of his voice, to be blunt, but because he looked so damn' macho and, well, sexy, in that get up. Confident of his effect on every woman in the theatre, complete with that stupid knife in his belt. Sex and violence; the irresistible combination. All I could think of at the time was God help all the women susceptible to music as well!' She stopped, her colour higher, her face ablaze with self-derision.

Honor sat back in her chair. 'Go on,' she said quietly, 'get it off your chest.'

'When he walked over to me on the stage, with everyone looking on, to me it seemed he was still performing. Can you understand? I didn't like being part of the act. Then when I realised he was the man I ran into in the park——'

'What? You mean the one in the mask?' Honor's eyebrows shot into her hair.

Judith nodded moodily. 'Yes. That's why he singled me out like that; to apologise.'

'Oh, I see.'

'It seemed urgent to let him know I wasn't one of his adoring fans—all those musical groupies that seem to hang round him everywhere, according to the Press.'

It was news to Honor that Judith had ever read anything about Rafael at all before yesterday's item on his hospitalisation. 'So you ran for home,' she said.

Judith gave a hard little laugh. 'The big joke, though, is that when I saw this man coming behind me I thought it was *him*—Rafael, for a split second; the great man himself, running after Judith Russell! I was brought down to earth pretty sharply, wasn't I? Quite literally!'

Honor touched Judith's hand soothingly. 'But darling, Rafael isn't exactly, well, how shall I put it— immune to your own particular attraction, shall we say? I can vouch for that personally. When he saw you lying unconscious——'

'I know, I know,' said Judith impatiently. 'You've told me he went all Latin and dramatic, but that illustrates exactly what I'm saying. Melodrama is his daily bread. How could one ever possibly know if he were really sincere?'

'When one knew him well enough, presumably.' Honor hesitated, then asked carefully, 'The evening you spent together at Gresham House, did you—I mean was there——'

'We walked in the garden,' said Judith evenly, 'and we sat in that rather fictitious looking pergola in the dusk. On a loveseat. Instead of singing a duet, as could reasonably be expected with such a setting, we told each other our life stories, and then the talking stopped and the lovemaking began. It would have progressed in a hurry to its natural conclusion, too, only he threw me down on the grass with rather too much enthusiasm and I hit my sore head. Saved by the bell, as it were. I was so crumpled and disreputable by this time that I had no alternative but to go to bed as an excuse to take off my dress. It was a mess. I wasn't ill at all when you came in, just suffering from frustrated libido!' Tears welled up in Judith's dark eyes, and began to trickle down her cheeks. 'And I haven't seen him since, Honor, or heard from him except for those damned carnations, and—and it *hurts!*'

'Oh, darling!' Honor rocked her in her arms, at a loss for a way to give comfort.

Judith pulled a crumpled wad of tissues from her pocket and mopped at her eyes. 'I thought I would at least be able to see him if he came back here, but now—now perhaps I'll never see him again.'

CHAPTER SIX

AFTERWARDS Judith was a little ashamed of her outburst, but in some ways it had acted as a necessary safety-valve for the feelings built up inside her like steam in a boiler. Unfortunately the aftermath was a bleak, desolate limbo, with no more daily carnations and no idea of where in the world Rafael might have taken himself off to lick his wounds. It was the not knowing which was so hard to bear. In vain she kept telling herself this feeling would eventually disappear and she would get over Rafael in time. A few hours together, a confidence or two, even some admittedly impassioned lovemaking, could hardly be counted as reasons for Rafael to reveal his whereabouts to her, much less his plans for the future. Reason with herself as much as she liked, Judith was nevertheless bitterly hurt by his silence, and had difficulty in hiding the fact from Honor.

As an antidote Judith threw herself into her work with whole-hearted concentration, trying to sublimate her hurt in sheer physical effort, and to some extent succeeded. Her leisure hours were more of a problem, with no Rob to help pass the time. Not that she missed Rob. Already it was difficult for Judith to remember him as anything but a passing acquaintance, even though he'd been her constant companion for almost a year and shared a great deal of common interests, both professional and social. By contrast the time spent with Rafael was minimal, yet he remained immovable in her mind, the memory of his lovemaking haunting her dreams. Diligently though Judith worked at trying to forget him, it was like giving up breathing for all the success she had.

Eventually Judith's annual holiday was due, and listlessly she mulled over the best way to spend it.

'Do you want to borrow the car? It's just passed its M.O.T. again,' said Honor.

'Could you spare it for a whole fortnight?' Judith's face lit up. 'That's exactly what I'd like. I could tour around a bit, and now the season's just about over I should be able to get bed and breakfast in most places, I think.'

'Where do you fancy?'

'I don't know. Not as far as Scotland; the Lake District maybe, or Wales.'

Next morning over breakfast and the Sunday papers Honor gave a little gasp and handed over a section of her paper to Judith. There was a short announcement in the arts section to the effect that due to indisposition Rafael David would not be appearing in the scheduled performance of *Carmen* the following month, and was resting indefinitely on the advice of his doctors. Judith met Honor's eyes in distress.

'What *is* the matter with him, Honor? Doesn't Martin know anything?'

Honor shook her head.

'He knows where Rafael is, but he's promised

faithfully to keep the location secret. All he will say is
that Rafael's operation was completely successful;
nothing malignant, if that's what's troubling you.'

'Everything's troubling me,' said Judith fiercely. 'But
if he wants to play Garbo there's not much point in
beating my head against a brick wall, is there? Never
mind, I'm off on my travels on Saturday, thanks to my
kind, lovely sister, and by the time I come back I
promise faithfully I'll have driven the wretched man
right out of my system—literally!'

'Big words, love. Let's hope you're right.' Honor
smiled doubtfully.

'And while I'm away you can ask Martin round for
cosy little candle-lit dinners, can't you?' Judith smiled
naughtily. 'While the cat's away, and all that!'

'He's taking me out to the theatre tomorrow night, in
fact,' said Honor, magnificently casual.

'Is he now!'

'*Henry the Fifth*, at the R.S.C.'

'You've kept that quiet!'

'He only got the tickets yesterday—from a friend
who can't go, so he's taking me, which is nice.' Honor
smiled ruefully. 'I didn't say anything last night,
because you were——'

'Such a moaning misery,' interrupted Judith in
remorse. 'I'll be better from now on, I promise. Have a
lovely time tomorrow, darling.'

It was after one in the morning by the time Honor
returned home after her night out. Nevertheless she
went straight up to Judith's room and shook her
gently.

'Judith, wake up.'

Judith scrambled upright in bed, rubbing her eyes.
She peered at her watch indignantly. 'It's past one—
what's the matter? Something wrong?'

'No, no, nothing wrong. Sorry about the time, but I
couldn't wait until the morning.'

'Martin's proposed!'

'Don't be silly, of course not,' said Honor, put out.
'It is a sort of message from Martin, though.'

Judith's eyes narrowed suspiciously. 'Oh yes? What sort of message?'

'He told me to say that the west coast of Wales is very beautiful, if you're undecided where to spend your holiday.' Honor met Judith's eyes very directly. 'He said not to miss a village called Morfa. There are a few of these dotted about Wales, I gather, but this one's on the coast somewhere between Aberystwyth and Cardigan.'

Judith looked at her in speculation.

'Does it have some special feature to recommend it, this Morfa?'

'Martin wouldn't say another word, so I didn't press him. He must think you'll like it there, I suppose.' Honor paused in the doorway. 'He did mention a nice pub where you might get a room. It's called the Anchor.' She smiled and said good night, leaving Judith very thoughtful as she settled back against her pillows. If this was where Rafael had gone to ground Martin obviously thought it a good idea for her to follow, to see how he was. Martin had kept his word in a way, not mentioning Rafael's name at all, merely extolling the virtues of Morfa. Even so, the possibility of Rafael's pleasure at seeing her, even if she did find him, seemed remote. Two brief encounters, a few kisses; hardly the basis for a relationship of any kind. But argue with herself as much as she liked, Judith knew very well that wild horses wouldn't keep her away from Morfa now. The trick would be to convince Rafael her presence there was a coincidence when she found him—and find him she would, or perish in the attempt.

Early Saturday morning Judith packed the car with a suitcase full of sensible clothes, added her Barbour jacket and green rubber boots, a cagoule and a bag of books and kissed Honor goodbye.

'Be good,' she told her cheerfully.

'And you be careful,' warned Honor. 'Did you remember a map?'

'Yes. I've tried to remember everything. I'll ring you from—wherever I get to tonight.' She smiled. They both knew very well Judith would be in Morfa by nightfall even if she had to walk there.

She rather wished she had as she guided the Morris at a snail's pace down the five miles of hairpin bends that led down from the main road to Morfa, which lay in a cove, a little nick in the coastline of Cardigan Bay. It was peaceful and very pleasing to the eye, she found, as the Morris squeezed down the steep road between sparkling clean cottages bright with immaculate paint. The commercial attractions appeared to consist only of a village shop, a small café with buckets and spades on sale, and finally the Anchor itself, a solid, weathered building crouched foursquare on the edge of the beach, looking out on a panorama of pebble-fringed sand and sculptured cliffs, with the blue sea beyond. Behind the inn the road rose sharply upwards again to disappear round the curves of fern-carpeted hillside which sheltered the Anchor from the east wind.

As Judith looked at the inn she felt a pang of doubt. It was by no means large, and if it were full there was no other place in Morfa to spend the night. Judith parked the Morris in the small car park adjoining the Anchor and got out, feeling stiff and hot. She went through the door of the pub, finding herself in a narrow passage separating two bars. The main, public bar lay to the left, already fairly full, and to the right lay the snug, more comfortable but less cheerful, and empty except for a quiet elderly couple gazing at the view over two glasses of lager. As she hesitated a door opened at the end of the passage and a thickset dark man emerged with a tray loaded with glasses. Hoping he was the landlord Judith smiled at him and said good evening.

'I was told you might be able to put me up,' she said hopefully.

'And who told you that, then, my lovely?' The man smiled back jovially. 'I'm happy to say we've been full up ever since Easter.'

Judith smiled ruefully. 'I should have realised, I suppose. Being late in the season I hoped——'

'Wait a minute, though.' He scratched his head. 'I

might manage something.' He called up the narrow
stairway. 'Mair! Is anything spare tonight?'

'Yes, Dad,' called a young, lilting voice. 'I told you
when the beer dray was here—didn't you hear me? The
Prossers arrived this afternoon without their eldest son;
only the little ones are with them. The top room is
spare.'

'There you are then, Miss . . .' He turned back to
Judith expectantly.

'Russell,' said Judith, smiling radiantly. 'Thank you
so much. I had no idea where to go otherwise—I'm very
grateful, Mr——'

'Owen Morris is my name. I run the place with the
help of my family. My wife does the cooking—nothing
fancy, mind, and Mair and Gareth help in the bar
and the house. How long were you wanting to stay,
then?'

'Could you manage two weeks?'

'Right you are. Only a small room, mind. I'll get
Mair to show you once we've seen to your luggage.'

The room *was* small, right up under the eaves, with a
single bed, a wardrobe, a small dressing table and stool,
all crammed in under the sloping ceiling, but the
window had a wonderful view, the mattress was
comfortable and covered by a woven Welsh quilt, and
the entire room was scrupulously clean. Judith smiled
warmly at the pretty teenager who'd shown her up.

'A bit small,' said the girl apologetically. 'Supper's
ready when you are. Mam won't call it dinner—says
that's too posh, but she's a good cook, I promise.'

Judith hurried down to the bathroom on the floor
below for a quick wash, then dashed back upstairs to
put on a clean white shirt and black linen trousers
before going in search of supper. The small dining room
was full, only a very small table near the door obviously
waiting for Judith. She tucked into her meal with
enthusiasm. After dinner she hesitated, wondering if it
were the done thing in these parts for a woman to sit
alone in the public bar, but her problem was solved by
an invitation to join the pleasant young couple at the
next table, Tony and Carol Thomas, both teachers from

Cardiff. They had been there for a week, and were able to supply Judith with a lot of useful information.

'What lies up the hill behind the pub?' she asked, accepting the lager Tony bought her.

'A very nice walk, or climb, rather. It's steep, but worth it at the top, the view's marvellous,' said Tony.

Judith made them drink up so she could pay for the next round of drinks, and offered one to Owen Morris behind the bar. He accepted readily.

'Couldn't help overhearing your conversation, Miss Russell. Not a reporter are you?'

Judith laughed. 'Afraid not. I'm a physiotherapist, actually.'

'I thought you might be after our celebrity.'

Judith swallowed a mouthful of lager. 'No,' she said steadily. 'I didn't know you had one.'

Tony leaned forward, grinning. 'Maybe she's not keen on music, Owen, being English. She may not have heard of Brynmor Tudor.'

Judith had heard of the Welsh baritone, but only vaguely, and for a moment her disappointment was keen. Then she dismissed it. Rafael would hardly take the trouble to hide himself down here and then broadcast the fact to the world at large.

'Brynmor Tudor lives here in Morfa, then?' she asked.

'The big house behind the stone walls at the top of the hill. Says he can shout his head off up there and not disturb a soul—pity you missed him, he was here about a week or so ago, then he went off to Cardiff,' said Owen.

Although she joined in the general conversation with the friendly company in the bar Judith's mind was secretly working furiously. Perhaps Rafael and Brynmor Tudor were friends. It seemed likely; they moved in the same musical circles, and perhaps it was his house that was Rafael's retreat. She would do her best to find out at the first possible opportunity. At stop-tap she went up to her little attic room, feeling tired after the long journey and the substantial meal provided by Mrs Morris. The bed proved to be as comfortable as it

looked, and she fell asleep quite quickly, comforted by
the thought that maybe Rafael was somewhere close at
hand, wherever it was.

After a large breakfast Judith dressed in a fleece-
lined track-suit over shorts and a sleeveless top, and
began to climb the hill behind the Anchor, striding
easily along the road that wound up the hill like a
helter-skelter slide around its tower. After a while the
road levelled out slightly and meandered along the cliff,
giving a breathtaking view of the sea below, the water
changing colour like a chameleon as the wind blew
clouds across the washed blue of the sky.

Judith paused, panting, to take in the scenery; the
village huddled far below, and above her the gorse and
ferns of the cliffs, studded here and there with an
isolated house. She carried a small rucksack on her
back, with a book, an apple and a can of lemonade,
intending to picnic and take full advantage of the long
walk if her search were fruitless. She decided she liked
the village very much. If Rafael was nowhere to be
found she might stay here just the same, lie on the
beach if the weather was kind, do some walking and
running; have herself a quiet, healthy holiday and put
all thoughts of him out of her head. But not yet. Not
until she had searched every nook and cranny of Morfa
first.

Judith set out again up the narrow road which soon
swerved upward and inland to climb the headland
above the bay, and toiled on until she reached a farm
track which forked off the steep, winding lane. At the
entrance to the track she found a sign on a post half-
buried in brambles, and was just able to make out the
word 'Brynmorfa', which sounded promising. She
hoisted her rucksack more securely and set off down the
ridged track. Casting a doubtful look at the sky, which
was suddenly dark and threatening, she broke into a
sprint as the first heavy drops of rain began to fall, and
in seconds she was soaked to the skin, annoyed with
herself for leaving her waterproof cagoule behind, but
brightening in spite of the downpour when she found
the bramble hedge gave way to a dry stone wall which

continued for some distance until she came to a white five-barred gate, firmly secured with padlock and chain.

Hunched against the driving rain, Judith peered at the house which stood behind the walls. It was larger than the others nearer the village; a grander relation, but built of the same stone, and in the same uncompromising form. Under a slate roof satin-dark with rain, the house stood foursquare, durable and hardy, impervious to wind and weather, with five sashed windows on the upper storey and four at ground level bisected by a small porch whose stout wooden door stood tightly shut under a white-painted canopy of wood. Judith slumped despondently against the gate, careless of the rain, disappointment permeating coldly right through to her bones. The house looked deserted, the windows closed and blank. Quite obviously no one was inside. So much for her hopes. She sniffed miserably as a few hot tears ran down her cheeks to mingle with the rain. Judith trudged a little further past the gate, skirting the high boundary wall of Brynmorfa's garden. The wall made it difficult to see the back of the house and the track eventually dwindled into a field which sloped down into a dingle behind Brynmorfa, leaving only a narrow footpath, slippery now with rain. With an effort Judith could just see the upper windows at the back by standing on tiptoe and craning her neck, and suddenly she sucked in her breath in excitement, her eyes lighting up. Two of the windows were open. Someone, whoever it might be, was in residence.

It could be a housekeeper, Judith warned herself. But the excitement deep inside her refused to admit the possibility. There was a gate in the wall, she found a moment later, with a circular wrought-iron handle. Judith turned it with caution but it moved only half way round and stuck. The gate was locked. She let out an explosive sigh. What should she do now? Judith looked at the wall with a measuring eye. It would take a pole vaulter to get over that. The rain was still sheeting down and belatedly Judith pulled the hood of her track suit top over her sodden head and pulled the drawstring tight. It seemed fairly obvious that the only way in to

Brynmorfa was over the five-barred gate, so she retraced her footsteps along the path and back along the track by the wall, then swung herself over the gate, landing on the path inside with a squelch of wet rubber on gravel.

'You! You are trespassing!' A tall, familiar figure shot round the corner of the house, and Judith's heart did a somersault. 'This is private property——' Rafael stopped as she threw back her head, pushing the hood from her hair.

'Hello, Rafael,' she said quietly, and slid the rucksack from her shoulders. 'I hoped you might be here.'

He stared at her thunderstruck, his curling black hair flattening in the downpour. 'Judith?' His voice was hoarse, angry, and there was no welcome on his face as the surprise faded. He looked gaunt, dark shadows under eyes that were unrecognisably dull. Suddenly he came alive to the rain and her sodden state. 'You had better come in,' he said ungraciously and peered behind her suspiciously. 'You are alone?'

'Yes,' said Judith meekly and followed him round the house. The back door stood open and he stood aside for her to enter a large, farmhouse-style kitchen where the cupboards and fittings had been chosen to blend with a Welsh oak dresser, and solid oak table and Windsor chairs. Judith stood dripping on the red-tiled floor, suffering from a strong sense of anticlimax and rebuff, as Rafael silently handed her a towel and rubbed at his own hair with another. Head on one side, he scrutinised her face with a look that seemed to assess her reasons for being there, and was obviously not intending to speak first. The whole scene was very little like she'd imagined. Unknown even to herself until this moment she had cherished a picture of being clasped to his broad chest, Rafael eloquent with gratitude for her arrival. Instead of which there was a distinct chill in the air, an indifference almost bordering on hostility.

'I'm on holiday,' she said lamely at last.

'Es verdad?' he said sardonically. 'And just by chance you happen to choose Morfa for your vacation!'

'Martin mentioned how beautiful it is in this part of the world so I decided to tour in Honor's car.' Judith put the towel down and took a comb from her rucksack, tugging it through her hair to avoid his eyes. 'How are you, Rafael?'

He lifted one shoulder in a negligent gesture. 'I *was* fine.'

Judith's eyes kindled. 'Until my intrusion, you mean.'

'Your words, Judith, not mine.' His gaze was mocking.

'Martin never actually mentioned your name,' she felt bound to point out. 'He merely extolled the peaceful attractions of Morfa and I did my own detective-work from there on. Did it never occur to you that everyone would be—concerned?'

'I needed to spend time alone,' he said bleakly. 'The life I lead . . .' His mouth tightened and he turned away to stare through the window. 'Let us say I have never had much opportunity to be alone. Bryn, the owner of this house, came to see me at the clinic and offered me the use of Brynmorfa for as long as I needed it. We drove down here with enough food for an army, and then he left me to it, as you say.'

'To what?' asked Judith bluntly.

'To the contemplation of my immortal soul, *querida*,' he said with sudden bite. 'Unlike you, Judith, I have difficulty in "keeping things light". You must blame the mixture of Spaniard and Celt in my blood.'

Impulsively Judith went to him, laying a hand on his bare forearm, but to her dismay he moved deliberately away.

'Was—was the operation unsuccessful then?' she asked with difficulty.

'Why no. It was very successful. The growth was not malignant, as at first feared. It was removed very efficiently and now I can even talk again; a little hoarsely, as you can hear, but it improves each day.'

Judith gazed at him unhappily, at a loss for something to say. It hardly seemed possible that this was the man who'd made love to her with such heat and sent flowers so extravagantly one by one. Wishing miserably she had never set foot in Morfa she picked up her rucksack.

'I'll be on my way, then,' she said stiffly. 'I'm glad you're better.' Not that he looked it. 'I'll tell Martin I saw you. Goodbye.'

Rafael moved swiftly to bar her way. 'You cannot walk down to the village like that. You must dry your clothes, have a hot bath——'

'No! Please. I'll only get wet again.' Judith side-stepped to pass him, but he shut the door and leaned against it.

'You might as well stay now you *are* here,' he said, the hoarseness of his voice so foreign from its normal vibrance.

She looked at his inscrutable face doubtfully, then shrugged.

'Requested with such charm how can I refuse?'

Rafael's face relaxed a little and he led the way from the room. Judith followed him upstairs to a large, recently modernised bathroom, obviously once a bedroom.

'Shall I try to find something for you to wear?' he asked politely.

'No, thank you. I'm wearing shorts and a top underneath; they should be all right.' She shivered suddenly. 'Perhaps a sweater, though—I'm a bit cold.'

'Yes, of course. Be quick, then.' Rafael closed the door and left her to strip off the wet track-suit. The shorts and top were a little damp, and she draped them on the radiator hoping they would dry while she was in the bath. She lay in the steaming water for ten blissful minutes or so before getting out reluctantly to towel herself dry. She put her black shorts and white cotton knit top back on. Her track shoes were sodden. Bare feet were preferable to squelching around in those, and she balanced the shoes carefully on the radiator and spread her track-suit to join them. As Judith combed the tangles from her damp hair in front of the mirror her reflection was something of a surprise. Even allowing for the effects of wind and rain there was an unusual glow on her face, her eyes bright with suppressed excitement. She gave herself a congratulatory smile; she had found Rafael, however cool his reception, and he had asked her to stay for a while too, which was a minor triumph.

To Judith's surprise Rafael was grilling some fish when she returned to the kitchen. The table was laid for two with a red-checked cloth, a basket of bread and a bowl of ready-tossed salad standing alongside a bottle of wine. He turned as she came in and gestured to a white sweater slung over the back of one of the chairs. His eyes flickered for an instant as they rested on her long brown legs and the clinging shirt, and he said brusquely.

'The sweater will be big, but I don't care to venture among Olwen Tudor's possessions. Also I thought you might be hungry; I have prepared lunch.'

'That's very kind of you,' she answered quietly, 'and the sweater will be fine.' In fact it was very large when she pulled it on, completely hiding her shorts from view, but she made no comment, smiling at him brightly. 'I'm much warmer now. The weather changed rather dramatically while I was on my way up here. It's quite a steep pull up from the village.'

'Is it? I wouldn't know.' Rafael turned back to the grill. 'I have never been down there. The road past the house also joins the Cardigan Road; it is unnecessary to go down into Morfa.'

'Oh, I see.' Which explained why his presence was unknown to the village. 'I heard in the Anchor that Brynmor Tudor was here recently,' said Judith. 'The landlord told me he had gone to Cardiff.'

'Bryn made a point of broadcasting the fact. So that I could be left in peace.' The dry sarcasm in Rafael's voice made Judith wince as he slid two large sizzling mackerel on to warmed plates with surprising deftness and carried them to the table.

'And at night?' she asked, sitting in the chair he held out for her. 'Aren't you afraid someone will see the lights?'

'The sitting-room and my bedroom are at the back. Besides, very few people ever pass this way at night.'

Gravely he offered her salad and poured wine into her glass. Judith tasted the fish and smiled across at him with surprised pleasure.

'This is delicious! I didn't know you could cook.'

'Why should you? We are virtual strangers, are we not?' The cool, quizzical look in his eyes chilled Judith.

'True,' she agreed, her smile fading. 'Where did the fish come from?'

Rafael jerked his head seawards. 'From down there in the bay, caught by Bryn himself and deep-frozen by his wife. Good, no?'

'Very good. So is the salad.' She smiled with deliberate friendliness, and some of the ice encasing him seemed to thaw as he looked at the long hair coiling damply over the wool of his own sweater.

'You look very young like that,' he said abruptly.

'I'm twenty-four,' she said, buttering a piece of bread. 'How old are you?'

'Thirty-nine.' Moodily he pushed his plate away and refilled their glasses. 'Centuries older than you in every way, Judith.'

'Age is a relative thing, Rafael—a state of mind, according to my mother.'

'You think so too?'

'Definitely. She has a habit of being annoyingly right.' Judith studied his sombre face, wondering just exactly how the operation had affected him. He was wearing an open-necked white shirt under a black sweater, but the blue cotton handkerchief knotted round his throat effectively hid any signs of a scar. He frowned as her eyes lingered on him.

'Why do you stare, Judith?'

She took the bull by the horns. 'I was wondering why you felt the need to hide away—to cut yourself off from all those who love you.'

Rafael's expressive mouth curled in derision as he sat twirling the stem of his wine-glass.

'And who are all these people who love me? The hangers-on who crowd around me at parties, enamoured by my success, my money; those who clamour for my autograph——'

'And buy your records and queue for hours to hear you sing,' put in Judith drily.

'Ah, but what about Rafael David the man?' he demanded, his voice raw as he leaned towards her. 'Not Don José, or Rudolpho or Faust, but *me*. The person behind the voice.'

'Well I, for one, had never really heard you sing before the concert in Hardwick,' said Judith matter-of-factly. 'Remember me? I'm one of the non-musical barbarians of the world!'

The brooding eyes softened a little.

'Yes. I remember well. You ran away to escape from me.'

'I wouldn't have put it quite like that. I meant that for me your musical side doesn't count very much, nor can you say it's the only bond between you and Martin, either. To him you're friend first and celebrity last.'

Rafael smiled faintly. 'Martin is different.'

'Then why wouldn't you stay with him to convalesce?' Judith persisted.

He lifted one shoulder in a bitter, expressive gesture. 'Because, *chica*, for once in my life I must struggle with this particular, private devil completely alone. No one can help me.'

Judith felt deflated, lacerated inwardly by the implication in his words. Her journey of discovery was shown up as nothing less than an intrusion after all, pointless and immature. She would have done better to leave him in peace.

'I'm sorry, Rafael. My intention was never to trespass on your privacy.' She rose briskly, avoiding his eyes as she took the lunch dishes to the sink. 'I—we were all worried. I just happened to have this holiday coming up, and Martin supplied me with a clue, so I gave in to impulse and followed it up.' She kept her back to him as she rinsed glasses and plates, stacking them with precision. 'I can tell Honor and Martin everything's fine, then, can I? Any messages?'

'You can give them my love,' he said huskily. 'Aunt Vinnie, too. Tell them—tell them that I need to put my house in order, I think you say.'

'I'll do that.' Judith dried the dishes rapidly and turned to face him, a polite smile firmly in place. 'There. Thank you so much for the lunch; now I think I'd better be on my way.' She pulled the sweater over her head and handed it to him, shivering a little without its warmth.

'Keep it on,' Rafael said brusquely, an odd expression on his face. 'You will catch cold.'

'No, I can't do that. I have no way of returning it.' Judith felt deeply depressed, and longed for escape; not only from Rafael, but from Morfa as well.

Rafael held out a hand in a gesture of appeal. 'Stay a little while longer. Drink coffee with me, Judith.' At once the roles were reversed. A surprising hint of entreaty lit Rafael's eyes with a little of their former lustre, and she responded to it involuntarily.

'I should go, Rafael.' She wavered visibly.

'Just for a few minutes, Judith.' His eyes held hers steadily.

'Just until my track-suit dries, then,' she said, capitulating.

He held out the sweater. 'Put it back on, *chica*.'

'I'm not cold—really.'

Rafael drew in a deep breath. 'Put it on, Judith, please. Your shirt is damp. It is clinging to your—your body. For my sake, if not for yours, cover yourself.'

Colour flamed in Judith's face and she dived hastily into the sweater, pulling it over her head with speed, rolling up the sleeves without looking at the man watching her, suddenly feeling all bare legs and untidy hair. Rafael turned away to fill a percolator, and with his back to her told her to go on ahead to the small sitting room across the hall. Judith went, glad to be alone for a moment, and curled up in one of the winged armchairs in the small cosy room, a copy of *Horse and Hound* open over her bare knees as camouflage by the time Rafael came in with a coffee tray.

'I have no cream,' he said as he put it down. 'Will you take it black?'

Judith nodded silently and accepted the strong, hot brew, sipping it quietly, conscious of Rafael's legs, clad in expensive black linen, stretching out in front of him opposite her.

'Are you cold?' he asked. 'I can light the fire——'

'No, really. I must be going soon.' Judith kept her eyes down, unwilling to meet Rafael's, but he leaned forward.

'How long will you stay in Morfa?' he asked.

'I don't know.'

'You are at the little inn there?'

'Yes. The Anchor.'

'Is it comfortable?'

'Very pleasant.'

'Did you get my flower each day?'

Judith's head jerked up, her eyes wide with surprise. 'What?'

Rafael leaned back, relaxed, an indulgent smile on his dark face.

'You heard me very well, Judith.'

Her chin lifted. 'Yes. I received the flowers. They've stopped coming now.'

'I know. I cancelled them.'

Judith regarded him thoughtfully. 'Why did you send them in the first place?'

'To be sure you did not forget me.' His face hardened. 'Then I decided it would be better if you did.'

'I see.' Judith's legs were cramped from their curled up position and she straightened them slowly, stretching them to relieve a slight ache. Rafael's eyes followed the movement intently, and very deliberately he leaned forward and ran his fingertip delicately from her ankle upward to the hem of her shorts. Judith's stomach muscles contracted and her lips parted as she stared at him in resentment. 'Why did you do that?' she demanded.

'To discover if your skin is as silken to the touch as it appears to the eye.' Rafael's voice was barely audible, and Judith stared, mesmerised, as the familiar brilliance returned to the eyes holding hers, their gleam hypnotic between the thick dark lashes. 'You should not have come, Judith,' he said softly.

'I know that,' she said flatly. 'I was a fool.'

'No, not a fool, Judith. A warm, caring woman, and I am sorry I gave you such a cold reception.'

'I understand, Rafael.' She jumped to her feet with decision. 'I'll leave now.'

He was before her, his hands on her shoulders.

'Don't go, Judith.'

She eyed him with distrust. 'You said you wanted to be alone.'

'I have changed my mind. I want you to stay. Please.'

'Why?'

'Because we—enjoy each other's company,' he said, with a cajoling note in his husky voice. 'The limited time we have spent together so far has not been enough. Stay and talk to me, Judith, please.'

'I thought you had your own personal private devil for company,' she retorted, still smarting from his earlier rebuff. 'What about him? Will he be one of the party?'

'Not if you stay. With you here perhaps I can forget him for a time.' There was an odd, wild light in his eyes that rang warning bells in Judith's head, but she chose deliberately to ignore them.

'All right,' she said casually, and released herself from his grip. 'Does that mean you're offering me dinner? I tend to eat rather a lot, I should warn you.'

Rafael laughed huskily, the first sound of genuine mirth she'd heard from him since her arrival. A warmth rushed through Judith involuntarily, and she grinned back at him.

'You may eat as much as you like, *chica*,' he assured her with a glint of white teeth, 'but only on condition that you cook it as well, unless you want the same as lunch—my culinary talent is very limited.'

'We can't all be perfect,' she said pertly.

'I try my best,' he said piously, and smiled, holding out a hand. 'Come. I will show you the giant freezer in what Bryn calls the "back kitchen". I think you say utility room, no?'

Giant was the word. Judith had never seen such a mammoth freezer. It was stocked with everything imaginable, from pheasant to blackcurrant pies. Judith

chose some lamb chops and put them to thaw, then
peeled potatoes for roasting, and decided on peas and
stuffed tomatoes to go with them. Rafael sat on the
kitchen table, legs swinging, and watched her, listening
with amusement to her account of her first day back at
work in the hospital, all traces of his earlier coolness
gone.

'My colleagues, to a woman, thought my grievous
bodily harm nothing against the thrill of being delivered
at Casualty by you,' she concluded, turning to smile at
him cheekily. 'It was the blood-stained frilly shirt that
really got everyone going, would you believe.'

'But yes. I still have it,' Rafael said solemnly.

'No doubt you do.'

'Unwashed, Judith—how could I bear to part with
your life-blood.' He laid a hand on his heart
dramatically.

'Ugh!' She threw a tea-towel at him, and he caught it
neatly, grinning. 'Do you have to be so melodramatic,
Rafael? I suppose the whole thing was just your cup of
tea.'

'I do not care for tea,' he said with dignity.

'You know very well what I mean,' Judith said
crossly. 'I have this feeling you're following a libretto
every now and then—it's very disconcerting.'

'But not dull!'

She regarded him thoughtfully, head on one side.

'No, Rafael; certainly not dull. In fact you might say
the even tenor of my existence has been severely
disrupted lately——' She gurgled suddenly. 'Did you
hear that, Rafael? That must be the only musical pun
I've made in my entire life!'

To her surprise there was no answering smile on his
face, which was suddenly suffused with a look of such
intense melancholy her smile died and she put out a
hand questioningly.

'I fear I am a very uneven tenor now, *querida*,' he
said hoarsely, and slid off the table, seizing her in his
arms. Instead of the kiss which she half expected he laid
his cheek against her hair and spoke rapidly in an
expressionless monotone. 'I had no intention—no desire

to speak of this, but I am not, and never can be, the
noble, silent type, Judith. For over half my life I have
made my living by expressing emotions through my
music, showing what I feel, suppressing very little. Oh
Judith, Judith, I did not mean to burden you with my
problem, but never in my wildest dreams did I imagine I
would see you here like this, and I find I cannot keep
silent. The operation has done permanent damage. I
can speak, but I cannot sing. At least not in the way
I could before. That is the particular devil who is to be
my life companion.'

CHAPTER SEVEN

JUDITH was stunned. She locked her arms round
Rafael's body in an agony of compassion. Tears
thickened her throat and she turned her head to rub her
cheek wordlessly against his. This had been her fear all
along, Martin's too, but to hear it as fact from Rafael's
lips was a shock to the system for which nothing could
have prepared her.

For a long time they stayed in silence, until she
finally asked,

'Did—did you know beforehand?'

'Yes. I had no choice. If the growth remained the
prognosis was—not good.' Rafael's arms tightened
convulsively. '*Dios*, Judith, what can I do with the rest
of my life? Without the voice I am nothing.'

Judith emerged from her anguish abruptly at this,
and held him at arms' length.

'Hey. Now come on—so you can't sing,' she said,
with brutal bluntness. 'It may be the end of your
particular world, but you'll just have to find another
world to interest you, that's all. Are you short of
money?' she added practically.

'No. I suppose I am a rich man. My mother left me
money as well as what I earn—have earned, myself.' He
stared at her like someone in shock, his eyes glazed, his

face devoid of colour beneath the olive skin. He flung away from her suddenly, his face angry. 'I was a fool to think you could understand. I was not referring to ways to earn my daily bread.'

Judith stood with arms folded, her eyes unwavering.

'I'm well aware of that, Rafael. And perhaps I don't understand fully. Music doesn't play any part in my life. And I know you're a big star, used to adulation and excitement. But in a few years or so you'd have to retire anyway, wouldn't you? It's come early for you, while you're right at the top of your particular tree—is that so bad? To be remembered always at the very height of your career?'

Rafael went over to the window, to stare unseeingly at the garden outside, his hands clenched at his sides.

'What I am trying to get through to you, Judith,' he said harshly, 'is that I have no idea how to occupy myself. I am not concerned for the moment with the things you mention. But my life is—was—filled to overflowing with rehearsals, recordings, incessant travel, interviews; many many things besides the actual performances. Without a voice all that is over. Finished. And my life stretches in front of me like a desert. I never married again after Lucia. I have no close family; all my friends, apart from Martin, are concerned with music. So what do I do? And when I come up with an answer, where shall I pursue this new occupation? In Granada—where people come to stare at my house because I was born there? Or in Milan, or New York or London, where people used to point me out in the street. If they did so now it would be with curiosity, even pity for a has-been.'

Judith had had enough.

'At least I now know the name of your private devil,' she said bitingly. 'It's self-pity. For God's sake get things into perspective, Rafael. You could have died— and spare me the "better if you had" bit! Quite a few singers have died with cancer of the throat; you were one of the lucky ones.'

'Your definition of luck does not coincide with mine,' he said coldly, not turning his head.

Judith ignored this. 'In my job I see a lot of people in pain, and sometimes nothing can be done and they die—young men in their teens, children too, who've never had a chance to live, let alone experience all the things you've packed into forty years of life——'

'Thirty-nine,' he muttered unexpectedly.

Judith cast her eyes heavenwards and went on doggedly.

'What I'm trying to say is that if you do sit on your rear end for the rest of your life, Rafael David, you have still achieved more than most. Not just the triumph and personal satisfaction for yourself, but all the wonderful pleasure you've given to the public with your voice—and will continue doing on recordings. Oh what's the use!' Judith gave up. 'I'm going back down to Morfa.'

'No!' Rafael leapt across the room and caught her as she made for the door. 'Don't go, Judith. Stay, please. For dinner, at least.' He bent gracefully and kissed her hand, looking up at her from beneath the celebrated slanting eyebrows. 'I do not know what to do with lamb chops.'

Judith was rather baffled by the abrupt *volte-face*. She looked at him thoughtfully as he straightened, at a loss how to respond.

'Very well,' she said unwillingly at last. 'But just for dinner. I must get back before dark—and I should let Owen Morris know at the Anchor. I said I'd be eating there tonight.'

Rafael waved a hand at the wall-telephone near the kitchen door.

'Please do. Then we find something pleasant and neutral to talk about, and spend a friendly hour or two together—no more heart-searching, I promise. I apologise for my lapse of control; a regrettable lack of your British stiff upper lip, no?'

Judith went over to the telephone without answering. Rafael leaned in the doorway, watching her as she spoke with Owen Morris, his eyes never leaving her face. She put the telephone back on its rest and turned to him, frowning.

'Why are you looking at me like that?'

He shrugged. 'I have been alone all week—and you are very easy to look at.'

'I'd appreciate the compliment rather more if it were my face you were looking at,' said Judith drily. 'I'll go up and see if my track-suit's dry.'

'Such a shame to hide those beautiful legs.' His smile flashed in the gloom. 'Do not be long then, Judith. We shall have a drink before you start demonstrating your culinary skill.'

They had more than one glass of the very dry sherry Rafael produced for an aperitif, and Judith began to feel warm and relaxed. They chatted comfortably together, like old friends, as she coped with the unfamiliar cooker, Rafael lounging in a kitchen chair, watching her supple, co-ordinated movements with enjoyment, and eventually Judith even confided her hopes on the subject of Honor and Martin.

'Don't you think it would be great for them both if they got married?' she asked. 'It seems such a waste for them to lead separate lives when I'm certain they're ideally suited to each other.' He smiled indulgently at her. 'Then perhaps you should tell them so. Martin is rather shy.'

Rafael proffered the sherry decanter. 'A little more?'

'If I do I'll never get the dinner to the table—I can only just about see straight as it is!' Judith grinned at him and turned back to the chops, then inspected the potatoes and tomatoes in the oven and put the peas to cook. 'Right, then. Five minutes and everything's ready.'

'Good. I am starving.' Rafael rose indolently to his feet, stretching like a great cat. He put out a hand to touch Judith's hair, but she dodged deftly, her cheeks flushed from the heat of the oven.

'No distracting the cook—and don't do a disappearing act just as I serve the meal, please!'

'With you, Judith, I put on no act, ever.' The effect of his words was rather spoiled by the dramatic hand he laid on his heart.

'You don't say!' Judith's eyes held a sceptical gleam.

'Yes, I do say. And I am your obedient servant, I promise—two minutes to wash, two minutes to open the wine,' he promised as he sauntered to the door, 'and afterwards I shall even wash the dishes.'

Judith smiled as he left the room, privately very doubtful that Rafael David had washed many plates during his celebrated career, though to do him justice the house was immaculate, as though he had taken pains to keep it in rigorous order during his time alone there. He returned quickly, as promised, and within minutes both were at the table before plates full of appetising food, their glasses filled with the smooth claret Rafael had produced as a suitable accompaniment to the lamb. He was extravagant with his compliments on Judith's cooking, his eyes sparkling wickedly as her colour rose when he said,

'So beautiful, and such a good cook also, Judith; what more could a man want? No other attributes are necessary!'

'Sexist!' she returned without heat, uneasily aware that her defences were by no means what they should be under the demoralising effect of the warmth and bonhomie prevalent in the atmosphere. She put a resolute hand over her glass as Rafael made to refill it. 'No more, or I shall never be able to walk back down to the village.'

'Then do not,' he said instantly, the levity suddenly gone. 'Stay here.'

Judith surveyed him dispassionately. 'And just exactly what do you mean by that?'

'What I say. Sleep here, then there is no necessity for you to walk back to Morfa.' He leaned towards her a little, communicating an urgency that made Judith retreat instinctively, wary of the immediate tension between them.

'And where would you want me to sleep, Rafael?' she asked bluntly. 'In your bed?'

Rafael's shoulder moved in the negligent gesture she was beginning to know well, and he got up to take their plates over to the sink. 'There are five bedrooms here, Judith,' he said over his shoulder. 'You can choose which one you like—including mine.'

Judith contemplated his broad shoulders thoughtfully. 'I'm not sure what you're suggesting.'

He swung round, his eyes unreadable. 'I am lonely,
Judith. When I first came here I craved solitude; I
needed very much to wrestle uninterrupted with my
problem. I was determined to stay here until I had come
to terms with being unable to sing. But now you have
changed all that. I detest the thought of being alone
again.' He spread his hands, a smile of self-derision
twisting his mouth. 'Not very heroic, am I? More a
child afraid of the dark. But I have need of your calm
good sense, *chica*. Stay with me. Please!'

Judith stared at him for a moment in silence, then
dropped her eyes, feeling uncertain and oddly gauche in
response to his intensity. 'I don't know that it's a very
good idea,' she murmured eventually.

'For you, no, I realise that,' he agreed. 'I am selfish
to ask you to give up your holiday.' He moved across
the room to turn her face up to his, meeting her eyes
with a look of such entreaty Judith's heart turned over.
'I will pay for the fortnight at the inn in the village. Tell
them you have been called away to a sick friend—not
so far removed from the truth, *querida*.'

'And what would I tell Honor?' asked Judith, but she
was wavering and a gleam of triumph lit Rafael's eyes
as he sensed victory and pressed home his advantage.

'Tell her the truth—that you are with me. She would
not give my secret away, I know.'

'She'll think I'm mad, and she's probably right, too.'
But Judith had given in and they both knew it. She
made one more protest as a face-saving gesture. 'Only
for a few days, then, Rafael.'

'I am in your hands, *Señorita* Russell—where are you
going?' as Judith jumped to her feet.

'I have to get back down to Morfa and then drive
back up that horrendous road, *amigo*, which is
something I'd like to accomplish before dark.' Judith
looked at Rafael steadily. 'I hope I shan't regret this,
Señor David.'

He bent his dark head and raised her hand to his lips,
a sincerity in the gesture which was oddly reassuring. 'I

shall endeavour to cause you no regret, I promise, Judith. I am grateful. *Muchas gracias.*' Rafael straightened, suddenly brisk. 'Now. I shall walk part of the way with you——'

'No,' she said at once. 'Someone will be sure to see you and then the hounds will be at your door. I shall run—it's all downhill. And I'll be back some time tonight in the car, if you'll tell me where to turn off the Cardigan road again—always supposing Honor's car ever makes it up those bends, that is!'

Rafael gave her precise instructions, the numb, dead look gone from his face, his entire manner changed as he instructed her repeatedly to be careful, then took a wallet from the pocket of his black cords and tried to give her money.

'No you don't,' said Judith firmly, stepping back. 'No money, Rafael. I'll pay my own bill.'

'But I wish to pay it for you,' he insisted, his face darkening.

'And I wish to pay it myself,' she countered steadily, 'or I don't come back.'

Their eyes clashed for a moment, then Rafael reluctantly replaced the wallet.

'Very well. You are very obstinate, Judith.'

'Yes—well, that's just one of the disadvantages you may have to accept with this situation.' Judith gave him a cheerful smile and took herself off, waving Rafael back into the house.

The rain had cleared, leaving a chilly, damp evening and Judith set off at a brisk pace down the winding road. The way back down to Morfa took much less time than the climb up, and she arrived at the Anchor sooner than expected, though a trifle more breathless than she would have preferred.

She found Owen Norris and explained that she was unable to stay after all, hurriedly assuring him that she would expect to pay the full amount nevertheless. He was shaking his head before Judith had finished speaking.

'A shame you have to leave, Miss Russell,' he said, 'but what's all this nonsense about paying for two weeks' board? One night you stayed, and one night you can pay for.'

'But I can't possibly do that,' said Judith quickly. 'I'd hate you to lose by it——'

There was a great deal of argument before the landlord was finally made to accept at least one week's payment to assuage Judith's conscience. She finally set out to negotiate the steep main street of Morfa, bracing herself for the ordeal of coaxing the Morris up the endless succession of bends that lay between the village and the Cardigan road. It took intense concentration and far more gear changing than the Morris cared for before Judith finally made it to the main highway, feeling limp with strain as she drove along it for the short distance to the turn-off Rafael had indicated. She turned down the narrow road and was obliged to slow down to a crawl to make out the bramble-disguised turning into the farm track. When Judith reached the gate it stood open, and Rafael appeared immediately at the sound of the car to close the gate behind her, waving her on towards the open door of a large double garage where Judith parked the Morris with great care alongside a black Lotus Elan that crouched, panther-like in the fading light.

'Nice little buggy,' commented Judith as she got out. 'Your get-away vehicle I presume.' She smiled at Rafael in greeting and gave the Morris a pat on its boot. 'What an incongruous pair!'

He laughed and took charge of her suitcase and parcel of books, locking the garage door and pocketing the key. 'Your little car has character, Judith.'

'You mean it's an old banger,' she retorted. 'And it's Honor's, not mine.'

Rafael ushered her into the house, locking the kitchen door behind him before going ahead of her through the hall and up the stairs. Judith followed the tall, powerful figure up to the landing, casting an eye round the various doors leading off it as Rafael stopped, turning to look at her with a smile in his eyes that showed he knew very well she was wondering about sleeping arrangements. He put her suitcase down and waved an arm around him.

'Three bedrooms at the front, two at the back, one of which is mine. You may choose which one you like.'

Judith gave an assessing look from beneath raised eyebrows, and went on a tour of inspection. Olwen Tudor had taste. All the rooms were furnished with maximum comfort, but in sympathy with the age and personality of the house. The larger bedroom at the front had its own bathroom and was the only double room; all the rest were single. Rafael's was the smallest and plainest, and it was obvious he had never intended Judith to share it, to her annoyance. The wicked glint in his eyes showed plainly he was aware of her irritation, and Judith decided it might be a good thing to put things straight. She leaned against the banister, arms folded, and looked up at him very directly.

'On the horrendous drive up from Morfa I had qualms, Rafael. On the face of it I think I must be mad to move in with you like this—we hardly know each other for one thing. And for another perhaps you ought to know that I don't make it a habit to go leaping into any old bed that's offered, either. In other words, it seemed more than likely that you might have the wrong idea.' She took in a deep breath. 'I've come because I honestly think you need someone right now. I know perfectly well there must be dozens of people only too willing to be with you, Rafael, but I happen to be the one on the spot it seems, so here I am. I'll cook, talk, play cards, sunbathe on the patio if the weather's good—I can even drive into Cardigan for supplies, if necessary. But I'm really not in the market for anything more—exciting, shall we say, than that. I thought I'd better make it clear from the start.'

Rafael stood fingering his jaw, a faint smile on his lips.

'Crystal clear, Judith. Possibly you misunderstood my sometimes ambiguous English when I offered you my room if you wished. I meant, of course, that I would move into another.'

'Did you indeed?' Judith looked at him levelly. 'Well,

I think I'll take the one at the other end of the landing at the back, but I'll use the bathroom in the master suite. That way we shouldn't get in each other's way at embarrassing moments.'

He laughed delightedly, and took her suitcase into the room of her choice.

'All will be as you say, *querida*, have no fears. Everything platonic and as decorous as though an army of maiden aunts were keeping watchful eyes on our every movement. Come down when you are ready—I shall make some coffee and give you a brandy to help you sleep.'

Judith was thoughtful as she unpacked. It had surely been best to put her cards on the table from the start, to leave no margin for error regarding her motives for moving in. It was an errand of mercy, nothing more— and it might be a very good thing if she were to keep that firmly in mind herself while she was on the subject.

Later that night Judith fell asleep almost as soon as she put her head on the pillow, worn out, one way and another, by the events of the day. Rafael had set out to be as charming and interesting as he knew how over their coffee and brandy, and an hour had gone by before either of them realised it was well after midnight. Judith had been sent off to bed while Rafael cleared away the tray, and there was consequently no constraint or awkwardness, as there might have been had they both gone upstairs together.

The following morning Judith woke with a raging headache and thirst, her skin burning and her throat dry and painful. With a groan of dismay she staggered to her feet, almost reeling as a wave of dizziness hit her. She struggled into her dressing gown and went across to the en suite bathroom, where she was promptly very ill indeed. Gasping and wretched she brushed her teeth, which were chattering so much the operation was by no means easy, and the reflection that stared at her, bleary- eyed, from the mirror was no comfort. Judith shuddered and stumbled back to her room, dragged a comb through her tangled hair and crawled back into bed, shivering violently. This was marvellous. What a stupid thing to happen. Judith was rarely ill, and, like all healthy people, felt it was the end of the world when laid low. In misery she lay, racked by tremors, her feet like blocks of ice and her head like a glass-blower's furnace. Apart from feeling so wretched she was consumed by angry frustration. The general idea was to knock Rafael into shape and get him back to normal again, and now it was she herself who felt like death warmed up, and hardly the most useful person to have around for anyone. In her misery Judith failed to hear the gentle knock on the door.

'Judith?' Rafael's voice was quiet, then became more insistent. 'Judith! Are you awake? It is past ten . . .' He opened the door a crack as she told him to come in, her voice so hoarse it was hardly recognisable. *'Querida!'* He moved quickly to the bed and laid a cool hand on her burning forehead. *'Dios*, you are burning up. You have a fever—I must call a doctor——'

'No, no,' croaked Judith crossly. 'Just give me a hot drink and see if there are any aspirin or something in the house. I've got a bit of a cold, or a chill, that's all.'

Rafael stared down at her flushed face in concern. He himself looked a lot better, in a crisp blue shirt and jeans that must have been tailored for him, Judith noted morosely, by the way they fitted him so well. The shadows under his eyes were less pronounced and he had lost the air of bitter depression that had surrounded him like an aura when she had first arrived. And now she was the casualty. They seemed to be taking it in turns.

'Are you sure, Judith?' he said at last, after Judith had forgotten what they were talking about in her misery.

'Sure of what?' She coughed irritably.

'That I should not call a doctor.'

'Very sure.'

'You were very wet yesterday. I feared this very thing—you should have taken off all those wet clothes immediately——'

'It didn't seem like a good idea at the time,' muttered Judith hoarsely.

Rafael bent to smooth her hair from her forehead. 'Can you eat, Judith?' His forehead was creased with worry as he examined her flushed face.

'No—thank you. Go away, Rafael.' She warded him off feebly. 'You'll catch it too.'

He gave a bleak little laugh. 'That is no longer of the prime importance it was once. I shall bring you a drink.'

Judith burrowed further under the covers and frankly gave herself up to her bone-racking discomfort. She ached everywhere. Even her teeth.

Rafael returned very quickly with a tray. 'I found some soluble aspirin, Judith, and here is some orange juice and then some coffee to drink afterwards.'

Obediently she drank the fizzing aspirin liquid, shuddering as Rafael sternly made her drain the last drop.

'Leave the juice for later,' she gasped. 'I'll just have the coffee.'

He regarded the thin satin straps of her nightgown with disapproval.

'You cannot be warm enough, Judith. Have you nothing more suitable for—for——'

'Feeling ghastly in?' She managed a crooked grin. 'There's a cotton sweatshirt in the top drawer of the chest.'

Rafael found the sweatshirt and helped Judith on with it, his touch impersonal as he tucked the duvet round her. She gave a sudden giggle, which promptly turned into another coughing fit.

'What is it?' he asked when she stopped.

Judith lay exhausted, her eyes mischievous beneath reddened lids.

'It suddenly struck me what a change it must be for you to be putting clothes on someone in bed—instead of taking them off!'

To her surprise he stiffened, his mouth tightening and his eyes glittering angrily. 'You have little idea of what is, or is not normal for me, Judith—and you were the one who vetoed such subjects.' He picked up the tray and went out.

Judith pulled a face and reached for the book on the bedside table, but the words danced crazily in front of her eyes and her head thumped, and her feet were still cold. The medication blunted the edge of her discomfort for a time but soon she was shivering again, her body aching dully, and the book slid to the floor with a bump. Within seconds Rafael burst through the door.

'What is it?' he demanded. 'Did you fall?'

She shook her head, trying to keep her teeth from chattering.

'The book did. God, Rafael, I'm so cold.'

'Wait there,' he ordered, and left the room at speed.

Where did he think she was likely to go? Judith had a shot at a smile, but her disorderly teeth made it impossible and she shed a few tears instead, wiping them away fiercely with her knuckles. That would teach her to go boring on to other people about self-pity.

Rafael came back in triumph, carrying a large, flat box and a clean sheet. 'I found it in my wardrobe—an electric overblanket, Judith.' He pulled the duvet from Judith's shivering body with speed, tucking the sheet around her before laying the electric blanket on top and plugging it in, finally adding the duvet. 'There, *chica*,' he said tenderly. 'You will feel warmer now.' He fished in the back pocket of his jeans. 'And here is a little silver bell. Ring when you want me, yes?'

'Yes,' said Judith, meek with gratitude as blissful warmth crept through her aching bones. 'Thank you so much, Rafael. I'm very sorry. I came to be a help and result in being a nuisance.'

'Nonsense, *querida*.' Rafael gave her one of his slanting, gleaming smiles. 'I needed something to occupy me, so now we play doctor and patient, a new game for me.'

A new game. Judith thought that one over at length when she was alone. Did Rafael think of everything in life as games to play or performances to act? She was still mulling it over as the warmth did its work and eventually she slid into an uneasy doze. When she woke she seemed to be on fire. The room was bright with sunshine, the bed was like a sauna and she was drenched from head to foot. She threw back the bedclothes and put her feet to the floor just as Rafael came through the door, his face stern.

'What are you doing out of bed?'

'I'm so hot,' gasped Judith, 'and I—I must go to the bathroom.'

Without a word he swung her up in his arms and carried her there, dumping her down inside the door with a curt order not to linger. When she walked slowly back towards her room she found the bed was stripped and Rafael was emerging from the door of the master bedroom.

'You can sleep in here, with your own bathroom at hand—no wandering about. I've switched on the blanket—have you another nightgown?'

Judith shook her head dumbly and submitted to being wrapped in a warm bath towel while Rafael disappeared again. This time he returned with one of his own shirts, a soft scarlet cotton knit.

'Put this on,' he said brusquely, and left while she did so.

Judith had no energy to argue. She did as she was told and climbed into the wide bed, feeling too wretched to care where she was or what she wore, still less what she looked like. Rafael appeared a second later with another dose of soluble aspirin, and she drank it obediently then settled back with a weary sigh.

'Thank you,' she said listlessly, unaware of the look of worry on Rafael's face as she turned her head into the pillow. The rest of the day passed in a blur of shivering and aching, of thirst and a cough that prevented her from sleeping even though she was never fully awake. When Judith eventually fell into a natural sleep she woke soon after, shivering again, her body so cold she could have been in a deep freeze. The room was in darkness and she fumbled for a light switch so she could turn on the electric blanket. Her fingers brushed against a metal object which fell to the floor with a tinkle. The bell. The sound brought Rafael to her side at the double, a candle in a brass holder in his hand.

'What is it, Judith? Do you feel worse?' He was in a dark dressing gown of some kind, the single, flickering flame accentuating the hollows and angles of his face, twin reflections of it in his eyes as he bent over her.

'No.' She smiled ruefully and raised a hand to push back her tangled hair, suddenly conscious of what a wreck she must be. 'It's just that I'm so cold again, Rafael. Would you switch the blanket on for me?'

'Alas, *querida*, there is a power failure. While you were sleeping we had a storm. It must have affected the electricity supply.' He shrugged, his white teeth catching in his bottom lip. 'I could fetch more blankets—no. Better I resort to an age-old but very effective way of keeping you warm.'

He blew out the candle, there was a slithering sound as the dressing gown slid to the floor and then he was in the bed beside her, pulling her against his warm chest and settling her head into the hollow of his shoulder.

Temporarily struck dumb Judith was quite unable to answer, even if she had been certain how to respond. She no longer felt ill, it was true. Her chill, fever or whatever had run its course, leaving her cold but very clear-headed. The cold feeling was dispelled at once by the nearness of the large, male body holding her close. There was very little bare skin in contact, due to her borrowed shirt and what were presumably his pyjama trousers, which fact made no difference at all to the excitement rising inside her; it affected her breathing, made her blood throb in her veins and filled her with an overpowering urge to press herself even closer to him.

'Well?' he prompted softly. 'Are you warmer now, Judith?'

'Yes,' she said breathlessly. 'But I'm not sure this is all that good an idea.'

'But effective!'

Which was true enough. Judith made a feeble attempt to move away, but his arms held her close, and she had no real desire to go far, anyway. It had been a token protest at best, and Rafael knew it.

'You see, Judith?' he whispered. 'The forces of nature conspire against you. It rains and you catch a chill; the lightning cuts off the electricity and there is no other way to keep warm than this—why try to fight kismet, *amada*? This is obviously where you are meant to be. Do you feel the same?'

Judith's body was in full agreement, but her brain had reservations.

'That's sophistry,' she said drowsily. 'You know very well you shouldn't be here.'

Rafael yawned suddenly and held her closer. 'I have no intention of returning to my cold lonely bed after tasting the delights of yours, *chica*, so resign yourself to the inevitable and settle down to sleep.'

Judith was in no physical state to oppose him for the moment so sensibly she did as he suggested, relaxing in the warm security of his arms, with only a fleeting thought as to the wisdom of giving in so easily. When she woke it was light and she was alone. The electric blanket was functioning and an edge of sunlight showed beneath the heavy curtains at the window. She frowned, almost ready to believe Rafael's presence had been a dream. Gingerly she turned her head and saw the dent in the pillow beside her—very close beside her. So hallucination was not one of her problems. The pressing one at the moment was the need for a bath and then food. She felt hollow and empty, as though her last meal had been days ago. Very carefully she swung her feet to the ground and stood up. Her knees were rubbery and she felt a bit limp, but otherwise all seemed to be well. She went into the bathroom, peering warily at herself in the mirror. She turned away in disgust to stand under the shower, massaging shampoo energetically into her sweat-soaked hair, enjoying the hot, cleansing water as it streamed over her body.

Afterwards Judith swathed a towel turbanwise round her head and wrapped herself in a large pink bath sheet. When she stepped into the bedroom she gave a small screech of fright. Rafael stood there, barring her way, looking like the demon king in a black track-suit, his eyes glittering balefully as they ran from Judith's damp turban to her bare toes.

'May I enquire what you are doing?' he asked politely.

'I would have thought it was fairly obvious.' Judith skirted him warily and made for the door.

'Where are you going now?' he demanded.

'To get some clothes from the other room—I can hardly wander round like this all day.'

'You should be in bed, Judith——' he began, frowning.

'On the contrary, I'm perfectly well now and I should be up and about,' contradicted Judith firmly. 'I'm as strong as a horse, honestly, and a few sniffs and a cough are hardly enough to lay me low, I assure you. I'm not accustomed to lying about in bed.' She gave him a friendly nod and retired hastily, away from the storm obviously gathering from the look on Rafael's face.

It took her only a few minutes to dress and quickly blow-dry her thick hair, revelling in the squeaky clean feel of it after the stickiness of the day before.   When she got downstairs she found Rafael in the kitchen, drinking coffee at the kitchen table. The scent of the fresh coffee was heavenly and Judith sniffed in rapture as he got up to pour a cup for her.

'I'll say good morning this time,' she said cheerfully, and glanced at the clock. 'Good heavens, it's only seven-thirty!'

'We are early,' he agreed. 'But you slept a great deal yesterday and I—woke early this morning.'

Judith felt her cheeks grow warm as she met the quizzical look in his eye.

'I'm sorry, Rafael. I suppose I was restless.'

He gave her a lopsided grin.

'No, Judith. *I* was the restless one.'

She regarded him calmly over the rim of her cup.

'I didn't know a thing about it. I slept like a log once—once I was warm.'

'Like an angel, *chica*, not a log. I watched you after I woke up.'

Judith glared at him.

'That wasn't fair! I must have been a sight—hair like greasy string and swollen eyelids—ugh!'

'You looked so horrible I was obliged to leave immediately,' Rafael agreed solemnly, looking into his coffee.

'Well thanks a lot!'

'*De nada.*' He smiled at her indulgently and got up. 'Are you hungry?'

'Starving! Shall I cook us something?'

'Not this morning. Breakfast I am good at, and I have prepared some of it already—Spanish omelettes, of course. You can make the toast.'

It was an effort not to wolf the food down when Rafael presented her with a golden omelette filled with potatoes, peppers, onions and tomatoes, bits of bacon and sausage, and Judith savoured the first mouthful with rapture.

'I thought you said you couldn't cook,' she said, mouth full.

'Basic things I can do. But more complicated dishes, with vegetables that must all be ready at the same time—this I find difficult. It is the timing.' He gave her a bright, topaz look across the table. 'Timing is very important, Judith, both on stage and off it, no?'

'I've never thought about it.' Judith refused to be diverted from enjoyment of her breakfast, and went on with her omelette, feeling better by the minute. 'Truly magnificent, Rafael,' she pronounced, as she finished the last mouthful. 'You can cook my breakfast any time.'

His eyes danced as he buttered a slice of toast.

'You must not say such things, Judith. They are bad for me.'

She smiled serenely. 'You know very well what I mean. I'm a very uncomplicated straightforward sort of person, you know, Rafael.'

'There is no such thing. All humans are complex.'

'Only some more so than others!'

'*Es verdad!*' They laughed together and Judith poured out fresh coffee.

'You were hungry too,' she commented, looking at his empty plate.

'Yesterday I was too anxious about you to think much about eating, and today I have been up since six.'

'Six! What on earth have you been doing since then?'

'Press-ups,' said Rafael, holding her eyes.

'For an hour or so?' Judith looked away, his bright, compelling gaze too much for her. Rafael shrugged, and leaned back in his chair.

'I cannot run here. I need the exercise. So I do press-ups—and skip.'

'Skip? Sounds fun.' Judith smiled. 'I'll join you when my legs feel more like mine again. At the moment they'd be more at home on a new-born foal.'

Rafael frowned. 'It is not surprising, Judith. You were not very well at all yesterday. I was on the point of ringing for a doctor several times.'

'I'm very glad you didn't. I'm basically very healthy, and strong. Which is just as well in my job.'

Rafael drew patterns on the cloth with the tip of his spoon. 'You like your job, Judith?'

She nodded, her eyes bright with enthusiasm. 'Yes. It's very satisfying. Most of the time, anyway. Usually I feel I'm helping people to feel better, move better, utilise their bodies properly. But occasionally I treat someone I know I can only supply with a little temporary relief, if any at all. I still get very depressed when I'm in contact with a terminal case, I'm afraid. Not so much now as in the beginning—one learns to be more objective, to keep part of oneself back.'

Rafael looked up quickly. 'And your doctor friend? Do you keep part of yourself back with him, too?'

Judith opened her mouth to say something cutting, then changed her mind, and shrugged. 'Perhaps that *was* the trouble,' she said reflectively. 'I was bringing the same detachment to personal relationships that I've been learning at the hospital.'

'Was?' pounced Rafael immediately. 'Is your *medico* no longer in attendance, then?'

Judith shook her head, avoiding his eye. 'No. He went off in a huff.'

'What is "huff"? You had a disagreement?'

'I suppose you could call it that. I—I wasn't romantic enough for him.'

Rafael's eyebrows rose. '*Lo siento*, Judith.' Not looking all that sorry as far as Judith could see.

'Don't be. I don't think I'm a very romantic type, really.' Judith got up and began to gather the dishes together.

'Everyone is romantic at some time or another; I refuse to believe you have no romance in your soul.' Rafael followed her over to the sink with the coffee tray and leaned against a counter top while she dealt with the plates.

'But then, your whole life has been spent in dishing it out on the stage,' she said tartly.

Rafael's face darkened. 'No longer, remember.'

'There's no point in getting all uptight again.' Judith looked at him militantly. 'We can't pretend you've never sung on a stage—it's better to talk about it naturally. I'm just not the type to go pussy-footing around trying to avoid the subject—I'd be sure to forget and open my big mouth at the wrong moment.'

To her relief he relaxed at once, turning very deliberately to stare at her lips. 'It is a very beautiful mouth, Judith. Do not insult it.'

'I'm glad you like it,' she said demurely. 'But to return to the matter in hand, I must admit that the sight of you on the stage of the Gresham Theatre with a flower in your hand and a dagger in your belt was enough to satisfy the most romantic of souls. You certainly got to me, and I'm not even a music lover!'

He frowned, puzzled as he picked up a cloth to dry the plates.

'But that is how I always sing the Flower Song, whether in concert or in the opera.'

'Yes, I assumed it was pretty routine for you, but I would be less than honest if I denied a very strong personal reaction,' said Judith candidly. 'As I said to Honor, sex and violence never fail.'

He laughed involuntarily, and reached over to give

her cheek a reproving pat. 'I think you make fun of me, Judith.'

'And it's very good for you,' she retorted, grinning. 'Too many women have been licking your handmade boots for far too long, Rafael David. It's time you had a change.'

'Ah, but why were they "licking my boots" as you put it, *querida*? If I had played second violin in the orchestra pit would there have been the same interest, do you suppose?' There was no bitterness this time, to her relief. His query seemed purely academic.

'But you wouldn't have been wearing a stiletto then, would you?' Judith giggled as he cast his eyes heavenwards before making a lunge and giving her a slap on her denim-covered behind. 'Ouch! That hurt——' Judith plucked a wooden spoon from a drawer and chased Rafael round the kitchen brandishing it until he backed up against the door with his hands in the air in grinning surrender.

All at once Judith was out of breath to her disgust, her knees buckling a little.

'What is it?' Rafael's laughter changed to concern and he pushed himself away from the door to turn her face up to his. 'Come—sit down, *chica*, you are not fully recovered yet, I think.'

Judith sighed impatiently and flopped down at the kitchen table, her eyes rueful as they met his. 'Obviously not. I'm not as fit as I thought.'

'Give yourself time, Judith. Yesterday you were quite ill; you cannot expect to be one hundred per cent fit so quickly.'

'No, I know. It's just that I hate having anything wrong with me.' She stopped, stricken, and could have bitten her tongue the moment the words were out as a shadow descended on Rafael's face. Impulsively she jumped to her feet and put a hand to his cheek. 'I warned you, Rafael. I'm not a bit tactful, but I really didn't mean to hurt——'

'Then kiss it better,' he said savagely, and pulled her against him, kissing her with a sudden ferocity that took her by surprise.

CHAPTER EIGHT

JUDITH struggled for only a moment, then gave in. Rafael's breath caught and he drew her even closer, bending over her, moulding her against the arch of his body, until with a sigh she melted against him in boneless reaction to his caressing mouth and tongue, kissing him back with an unashamed ardour that sent tremors through his body she could feel right through her own. At last he tore his mouth away and pressed her head against his shoulder, his breath rasping through his chest.

'*Querida*, I apologise, I am sorry. *Dios*, no, I am not sorry—to kiss you is a delight, but I know myself. I would want more; all of you, Judith, so run away quickly, while you can.' Rafael's arms slackened and Judith stepped back, looking up at him, her dark eyes considering. His own eyes blazed back at her. Colour tinged the olive skin that was taut along his jaw with the self-control he was exerting over himself. She felt a surge of triumph. Here was a different man from the recluse of two days ago. She could sense the tension in his body, and he was breathing unevenly, but the lack-lustre numbness was gone. Life and vitality vibrated from every pore again. Judith's mind ticked over at a furious rate as she looked at him in silence while her own breathing slowed. Was this what it took to bring him back to life? Mere physical contact with a woman? And if so could it have been any woman, or was it just remotely possible it could be herself?

'I don't want to go, Rafael,' she said at last. 'Must I?'

'It would be wiser, Judith.' A pulse throbbed at the corner of his wide, expressive mouth, and he stiffened as she moved closer to him again. 'Judith,' he warned, 'must I explain in more basic terms? For various reasons it is a long time since I made love to a woman, and to have you here alone like this—it is not—not easy. I should not have asked you to stay, it was sheer self-indulgence.'

Judith retreated obediently, seating herself on the table, long legs swinging idly. 'Do you feel better since my arrival, Rafael?' she asked.

'You know very well that I do.' He flung round and stared through the window at the windswept patio. 'But you must not regard yourself as someone with a mission, Judith. I must learn to recover, to re-shape my life on my own. You are young; you have your own life to live. I was selfish, crazy to suggest you stay here. Go back to Hardwick and forget about me.'

Judith scowled at his back in exasperation. 'My God, Rafael, can't you come off the stage for a bit? I know your stupid operas are choc-a-bloc with sacrifice and unhappy endings, but this is the *real* world. I'm not offering myself as a virgin sacrifice on the altar of your rehabilitation programme, merely as a companion to help you stave off the blues you were very obviously wallowing in when I arrived.'

With his back still obstinately turned Rafael began to speak rapidly, his voice suddenly hoarse again. 'You made things clear when you arrived, Judith. Everything platonic and laid back, with no sexual overtones.' Suddenly he thrust both hands into his thick black hair. 'It is different for a man, you little idiot—I cannot look across the table at you without thinking how beautiful those great dark eyes are, how shining and soft your hair. I want to touch your skin, have you near to me all the time. Call it emotional, melodramatic if you like. But that's the way it is; the way I am.'

Judith's anger died. She slid off the table and went to stand beside him at the window. 'Was that the reason for the press-ups this morning?' she asked softly.

The tension visibly drained from Rafael at the tone of her voice, and he turned to her with a rueful smile. 'They did not help nearly as much as they should have, alas!' He laughed, his good humour restored. 'Once again I apologise, Judith. I was—was frustrated, and I lashed out at you.'

'So can I stay?' she challenged him, her eyes impudent.

He spread his hands in an eloquent gesture of resignation, his teeth a sudden flash of white in his dark face. 'If you really want to, Judith.'

She nodded with assurance. 'Yes. I really want to. Besides I can hardly turn up at the Anchor again, so where would I spend my holiday?'

'You should be lying on a sunlit beach in Spain or Portugal, *querida*.' Rafael grimaced as he went over to fill the percolator. 'This part of Wales is beautiful, but a trifle cold for my taste in September.'

'That's your Latin blood complaining,' laughed Judith, taking down pottery mugs from a cupboard. 'Besides it's pretty windy up here, and these old cottages have such thick stone walls.'

'Which has given me an idea of how to occupy myself, as well as repay Bryn in some small measure for the loan of his house.' Rafael gave her rather a smug smile, obviously pleased with himself. 'At the back of the house there is a small valley with a stream running through it.'

'A dingle.'

'Dingle? Yes? After the recent storm there are branches and wood scattered in all directions, so I shall bring it up little by little to the woodstore and chop it up into logs and kindling for Olwen's fireplace.' Rafael poured a strong, black brew into their mugs, looking up at Judith with a gleam in his eyes. 'It will also serve to channel the surplus energy I never suspected had returned in such force since my stay in the clinic.'

'The human body has remarkable recuperative powers.' Judith eyed him with a clinical look. 'And yours should be ultra rapid, judging by your passion for exercise. I thought all singers ran to fat.'

'I jog instead—perhaps I'll get fat later.'

'Salad for lunch then. Now let's go and inspect the dingle, I can give you a hand——'

'Oh no. You are still recovering from your chill, little invalid. You prepare the lunch, I gather the wood; fair distribution of labour, no? You can help when you feel stronger.' Rafael was smiling, but there was a steely glint in his eye which Judith resented a little, but good sense prevailed and she nodded philosophically.

'O.K. But don't you overdo it either. You're still fairly convalescent yourself.'

Rafael shrugged indifferently at this, and peered at the unsettled sky. 'I'd better make a start, it looks like rain.' He went off to collect a sweater and went out with a casual wave, leaving Judith to tidy up the house. She made her bed, hesitated, then went along to Rafael's room to make his, but it was already done, the room tidy, bare of nearly all signs of occupation. The only personal possessions in view were a Walkman cassette player with accompanying pile of tapes, and a silver-framed photograph on the dressing table. Judith picked it up and looked at a young woman with hair drawn back into a knot, her eyes large and luminous in the pure oval of her face. The photograph was in black and white and Judith stared at it in fascination. Was this Lucia? And if so why did Rafael keep her beside his bed? A sharp little pang of jealousy stung her and Judith put the portrait down and hurried from the room, running down the steep stairs to whisk a duster round Olwen Tudor's small, cosy sitting-room.

At intervals she could see Rafael returning through the gate in the back wall with a barrow full of wood, emptying it out on the space in front of the woodstore near the garage. He was obviously a man of his word, and meant to keep on at his self-imposed task until he dropped, by the look of it. Judith smiled wryly and began to prepare a salad, and after some thought made some quenelles from a tin of salmon from the store cupboard in the 'back kitchen', where enough tins and dry goods were stored to see them through a siege. To her delight there was a small sheltered herb garden at the side of the house when she went exploring, and she was able to salvage the last of the parsley to add to her quenelles and flavour the sauce she intended to serve with them. Rafael seemed likely to be in need of something fairly substantial after his labours so Judith made a jam sponge pudding and put it to steam, then had thoughts about dinner, eventually taking two sirloin steaks from the freezer and leaving them to thaw while she prepared lunch. When the quenelles were ready, sautéed to crisp perfection, she gave Rafael a shout from the window as he emptied out a load of wood.

'Lunch-time—hurry up.'

He looked up, pushing the hair from his eyes with a grimy hand, then stretched, wincing a little as he strolled into the kitchen, sniffing the air with anticipation.

'Something smells good. I warn you I am starving, so I hope you prepared a great deal of food.'

'Enough,' said Judith briskly. 'Now have a wash in here so you won't mess up the bathrooms—I've just cleaned them.'

Rafael did as he was bid with mock subservience. '*Sí, señorita*. Is this how you order your poor patients about?'

'No indeed. With them I am all sympathy and compassion—do get a move on, or my quenelles will be spoiled.'

The emotional scene of the morning might never have happened. They talked easily over the meal, Rafael consuming a gratifying amount of food, including second helpings and most of the pudding.

'I have not eaten this before. It is very British, Judith?'

'Very. Nursery fare. And you wouldn't be eating it now if you didn't intend chopping all that wood up this afternoon—too many calories.'

Rafael pulled a face. 'Are you so concerned with my weight?'

'You were the one who said you might get fat.'

'And then you would love me no more!' In mock tragedy Rafael folded his hands together and cast down his eyes in a look of such utter despair Judith had a sudden vivid glimpse of his supreme artistry.

'Who's that?' she asked drily. 'Otello?'

'Or Cavaradossi, or Don José again, if you like.' His

face was full of laughter again in an instant and Judith shook her head in wonder.

'How can one ever be sure how you really feel, Rafael? With you it's impossible to tell whether the curtain's up or one's behind the scenes.'

Rafael drank the last of his coffee and stood up, biting his lip as he flexed his shoulder muscles.

'You should know better than most, Judith. I display my soul to you with rather disturbing frequency for such a short acquaintance, no? Believe it or not it is by no means a habit of mine.'

'Why me?' she asked quietly.

He shrugged. '*Quien sabe?* Although you are so strong and independent I have seen you wounded and ill, and in need of care and protection. Perhaps you appeal to the paternal in me.'

'Great,' she said glumly. 'That doesn't do much for my self-esteem, *amigo*.'

He bent to turn up her downcast face with his forefinger, placing a chaste fatherly kiss on her brow.

'At the present time, *chiquita*, my concern is with my own peace of mind. Your self-esteem must take care of itself.' He smiled into Judith's affronted eyes and went off whistling to make a further attack on the wood. The tune he whistled was familiar. Even Judith could easily identify it as the Flower Song from *Carmen*.

All afternoon Rafael hacked and chopped until the Tudors' woodstore was overflowing. Judith took him a tankard of beer halfway through and looked at him anxiously.

'Aren't you overdoing it a bit, Rafael?'

'No. In fact I'm rather enjoying it.' He was stripped to the waist by this time, his bronzed torso glistening with sweat and the curls of dark hair on his chest tangled with moisture. He drained the tankard gratefully and handed it back. '*Muchas gracias, señorita.*'

'A pleasure.' Judith frowned a little. 'I do wish you'd let me help.'

Rafael shook his head emphatically and picked up the axe. 'You may practice your equality elsewhere.

This is one job I firmly believe should be left to a man.'

Judith left him to it, privately considering him way over the top to attempt the whole lot in one day. He was certain to feel very stiff and sore afterwards, but she knew it was pointless to argue. When he eventually called it a day Rafael looked utterly exhausted when he came in.

'You are pig-headed,' said Judith severely, as he closed the kitchen door behind him. Rafael yawned mightily and stretched, his face contorting as his muscles protested.

'Pig-headed? Ugh!'

'It means you're very obstinate,' she said impatiently. 'You must be worn out—anyone would be. Have a really hot bath and stay soaking in it for a while.'

'A seductive suggestion.' He made for the door, patting her cheek as he passed. 'What's for dinner?'

'Is eating all you think about——' began Judith.

'No, *chica*,' he said at once, with an evil leer. 'I think of other things too. But you know about that already, no?' With an outrageous wink he left the room and went upstairs, whistling again. Judith listened carefully; not the Flower Song this time, too catchy to be opera, but nothing she knew.

Later, as Judith was putting the steaks under the grill, Rafael sauntered into the kitchen with a decanter and two glasses and filled one with sherry for her before sitting at the kitchen table to watch her. She was wearing a shiny plastic apron discovered in one of the drawers, bright red with a huge green apple painted on the bib, and Rafael examined it with amusement as she laid a yellow linen cloth on the table, and gave him a handful of cutlery to set out.

'If I was Otello earlier, Judith, is your role Eve?'

'And if it were,' she countered with a sparkling look, 'who would you be? Adam or the serpent?'

Rafael laughed, then sniffed ecstatically as the scent of grilling steak and mushrooms filled the kitchen. He eyed the crusty loaf and salty Welsh butter on the table beside him.

'May I have some of this, Judith? I am ravenous!'

'As long as it doesn't spoil your appetite; I'd hate my efforts to be in vain.'

'Nothing could spoil my appetite—I could eat a horse, saddle and all.' He seized the loaf and hacked off a thick slice, buttering it liberally. 'Let me fill your glass, Judith—or shall I open some wine to eat with the meal?'

'Not for me, the sherry's fine.' Judith accepted a refill, turned the heat down above the steaks and filled two pottery bowls with thick vegetable soup. She put them on the table and sat down.

'How's that? I thought you might like something filling tonight after your marathon lumberjack act,' she announced, smiling at him.

Rafael gave a sigh of pure pleasure after the first savoury mouthful.

'Judith, this is superb!'

'Hunger's the best sauce, my mother says.'

'What is your mother like?' asked Rafael with interest.

Judith laughed, and told him about her parents and their household, her mother's crime novels. 'I was with them just recently, actually. I went down for a weekend after—after——'

Rafael bent his head to look into her face.

'After what, Judith?'

She looked up at him without evasion.

'After your memorable visit to Hardwick.'

'Was it so memorable?' he asked softly, his eyes holding hers.

'I think you know very well that it was—one way and another.' Judith collected their empty bowls and took them away. 'It was while I was with my parents that I read about your operation. It was quite a shock to see it in black and white in the Sunday papers, coming so soon after——'

'After our time together in Martin's garden?'

Judith nodded, keeping her back to him, and he sprang up to help her, choking back a groan as he moved too suddenly. She handed him a sauceboat and the dish of savoury rice, then slid the steaks on to hot plates, garnished them with the mushrooms and followed him to the table. Rafael waited for Judith to serve herself, then took liberal portions of rice and fragrant tomato sauce, his appreciation highly gratifying to Judith.

'I am running out of English adjectives,' he declared, waving his fork. 'I thought youngsters like you lived off hamburgers and kebabs.'

'I'm hardly a teenager, Grandpa,' said Judith drily. 'And I ate my share of junk food during my training to vary the stodge dished out to us. I put on about twenty pounds in the first few months. It took an awful lot of will-power and teeth-gritting to get rid of them, I assure you.'

'You cannot feel regret for the effort when the result is so spectacular,' said Rafael, a light in his eye that brought the warmth to Judith's face. She went on with her dinner, keeping her eyes on her plate as she hurriedly went on with the conversation.

'I share the cooking with Honor at the cottage, of course.'

'My mother liked to cook also.' Rafael helped himself to more rice and sauce. 'Not as much as she liked because of her profession, and of course there was not the necessity. We lived in my gradparents' house, where there were servants. But after her retirement, when I was at home she would make paella as no one has ever made it for me since.'

'You loved your mother very much, Rafael?'

'Very much,' he said simply. 'She was a beautiful lady, both spiritually and physically. I have a photograph of her upstairs; I will show it to you later.'

Judith felt both guilty and relieved. So the portrait had been of Carmelita, not Lucia.

'She was one of the greatest Carmens ever heard in the role,' went on Rafael a fond, distant look in his translucent eyes. 'The stiletto you saw was hers. She always wore it to play Carmen, and the first time I sang Don José she gave it to me for luck and I never sing— sang the role without it.'

Judith stilled as he changed the verb to the past tense, but he appeared to take it in his stride, finishing the last of the food on his plate and putting down his knife and fork with a sigh of repletion.

'I didn't make a pudding tonight,' she said apologetically.

'How lazy!' He grinned at her boyishly. 'Is there possibly some cheese?'

Judith smiled back, a dimple showing in one cheek. He leaned forward and touched a finger to it gently.

'I very much like your dimple.'

'I'm pleased you're pleased,' she said demurely and went to fetch a bowl of apples and some Cambozola, the creamy, blue-veined Brie-type cheese she had found in the refrigerator, to her delight. 'I adore this stuff, Rafael. I can get frankly greedy about it.'

His eyes travelled over her with slow appreciation.

'I would never guess, *chica*. Your body is beautiful.'

Judith frowned as she spread cheese on a wholewheat biscuit. 'You should say "figure". "Body" sounds a trifle personal.'

'English is not my first language,' he reminded her. 'Nor my second, to be accurate.'

'Which is your second one, then?' Judith's interest was immediate.

'Italian, of course. The language of the opera.'

'How many languages do you speak?'

'I *speak* Italian, English and French, and less fluently German. But I can sing in a few other tongues also— sufficiently well to interpret the roles, at least.'

'You've left out Spanish.'

'I wished to impress.'

'You succeeded.'

Their eyes held for a moment before Judith's dropped. If Rafael were allowed to look into them for too long she had the feeling he might see right through into her mind, discover just exactly what was going on in her head, which would be disastrous. Increasingly she was aware that her inner defences were a shaky, crumbling edifice, with no proof against the strength of the feelings battering against them, a fact it seemed preferable to conceal from him at all costs. At the mere thought of what might happen if Rafael suspected the truth Judith swallowed hard and jumped to her feet precipitately.

'I shall help you to clear up,' said Rafael with determination.

'No! No—really.' Judith shooed him towards the door. 'You've been working hard all day. Go and watch some television or listen to music. I'll be no time at all.'

Which proved rather an optimistic estimate. Even with Rafael out of the way Judith was un-characteristically clumsy, all thumbs; quite the reverse of her usual efficient self. It was half an hour or more before she finally carried the coffee tray into the other room, feeling distinctly weary. Rafael switched off the symphony concert he was listening to and put a cassette of light, lilting music on Bryn's stereo system.

'That sounds like the tune you were whistling as you went upstairs,' commented Judith as she handed him his coffee.

Rafael gave her a look of limpid innocence. 'I believe the English translation is something like "Girls were made to love and kiss".'

'Is it really?' said Judith astringently.

'Music is nearly always inspired by love, or conflict of some kind, Judith.'

'Right back with the sex and violence again!'

He shrugged indolently. 'Human nature, *querida*.' He took a box from the small table beside him. 'I found this while I was looking through Bryn's records, Judith. Do you play backgammon?'

'Do I!' Judith's eyes lit up. 'It was the in-game when I was at the Nuffield.'

'Martin taught me to play years ago. Would you like to play?'

Judith nodded eagerly. Not only did she enjoy the game, but it seemed like the perfect solution as to how to pass an evening without getting into troubled waters. The memory of the morning's incident still lingered at the back of her mind, and every so often she was obliged to blank out thoughts of a hard, warm body against her own in bed the night before. Playing backgammon for the evening was a safer prospect than that other game for two Rafael had once mentioned with such vehemence.

They proved to be worthy opponents. After an hour or so the honours were even, with one game apiece, and Judith agreed readily when Rafael suggested a final game as decider.

'To make it interesting let us play for some kind of stake,' he said casually. 'If I win what will you give me as a prize?'

Judith stared at him sardonically. 'Had you something in mind?'

'No. Whoever wins can suggest the prize, no?'

'No,' said Judith consideringly. 'I think it would be more fun if whoever loses chooses the prize.'

Which transformed the deciding game into a battle of reversed strategy. At first however hard Judith tried to play badly the dice seemed loaded against her. She threw double sixes with infuriating regularity and found it impossible not to take Rafael's men, then slowly the tide began to turn. The overt triumph on Rafael's face darkened to frowning concentration as he tried in vain to maintain his losing streak. The final result was close, but in the end, after nearly an hour of inspired gamesmanship, he won—and lost. He replaced the counters and dice in the leather box and looked in enquiry at Judith, an expectant gleam in the jewel-like eyes.

'Can you think of anything I would like, *querida?*'

Judith smiled nastily. 'I think I can, Rafael. By morning I'm certain you'll be in crying need of my professional services, so as your prize you can have a professional massage and . . .'

The dismay on his face was too much for Judith. She gave way to helpless laughter, tucking her long legs beneath her and turning her head into the sofa cushion in abandon. Rafael's eyes kindled angrily as he watched her.

'And you think I might not enjoy that?' he asked silkily.

Judith recovered herself at once. 'Not as much as you might think, I'm afraid.'

He rose nonchalantly to his feet, only the set of his mouth showing the effort it cost him to do so without wincing. 'Then I shall retire at once so that these delights will come all the sooner—little tease.'

'I am *not* a tease,' she retorted hotly. 'Nor am I very little, if it comes to that.'

His eyes softened as they rested on her indignant face.

'You are young, *querida*. To an old warhorse like me you are a mere child.'

Judith jumped up impatiently. 'Honestly, Rafael, you drive me up the wall! You know damn well you're a virile, gorgeous man in his prime—and I'm not little Red Riding Hood—I'm an adult, self-sufficient, self-supporting woman, in case you hadn't noticed.'

'Judith, Judith—do not fly at me.' He backed away, hands up in mock surrender. 'Let us say good night before there is bloodshed.'

'I'm sorry,' she sighed, calming down. 'But stop putting on an act with me, Rafael. I'm not interested in Otello, or the other chap, or even in Don José, no matter how fascinating you made him. It's Rafael David the man who interests me, not because he sings, or because he's famous or rich, but because he's having a rough time and I want to help.'

Rafael's face emptied of animation as he stared at the passionate sincerity in her face.

'I am me, Judith,' he said heavily at last. 'I am what my life has made me. I am too old to change, I think.'

Judith took in a deep breath and let it out very slowly before smiling brightly at him. 'No. Of course not—silly of me. I was over-reacting. Good night. Sleep well.'

'*Buenas noches*, Judith.'

She turned in the doorway and smiled, catching her breath at the sudden blaze that flared in his eyes as they met hers across the room. Her smile faltered and she left quickly, instinct telling her to get away from there as fast as her legs could carry her.

CHAPTER NINE

THE sky was overcast and dull, with a strong wind blustering from the sea when Judith woke early the following morning. The house was very quiet.

She stole down the stairs. There was no sign of Rafael, so Judith made herself toast and sat down at the table to eat it with a mug of tea and a novel she had chosen from the bookshelf in her bedroom. She was not bored, she found—far from it. It surprised her, in actual fact, to find the enforced captivity had failed to give her a longing for escape. She had been ill for a day, admittedly, but even so, spending the hours with Rafael, playing at domesticity, seemed enough to absorb her energies completely for the time being. She wondered how he was this morning. Superb physical specimen though he was, after all the violent exercise of yesterday he might very well be feeling very sorry for himself.

It was some time later when she finally heard movement and water running in the bathroom. Eventually a door closed and there was silence again. What now? Judith remained where she was for a time, but after a while curiosity got the better of her. She ran upstairs and tapped on Rafael's door, opening it when his voice answered hoarsely. He was lying against pillows propped against the headboard of the bed, the duvet over the lower half of his body, his broad, flat-muscled torso bare. His thick hair was wildly tousled, and a dark growth of stubble shadowed his chin below tightly compressed lips, his scar showing redly on his throat.

'Do not be afraid, Red Riding Hood,' he said huskily, his eyes sardonic. 'You may enter without fear—I am barely able to move, so your virtue will go unmolested.'

Judith quelled a smile. 'Good morning, Rafael,' she said briskly, and went over to the bed. 'A bit stiff this morning, are we?'

'*I*, not we—and you may have the satisfaction of saying you told me so,' he said bitterly.

'But think of the consoling glow, the virtue of knowing you've filled the Tudors' woodstore for them,' she said with sweet malice.

'And virtue must be its own reward, I suppose?' A faint glint showed in his eyes, then dulled as he tried to move. 'The virtue, my dear Miss Russell, was not in the actual deed, but in the motive.'

'To repay the Tudors for the loan of their house?'

Rafael eyed her with malevolence. 'No! To sublimate those desires that otherwise might have been channelled in your direction.' He shifted his position a little, groaning dramatically. 'I succeeded beyond my wildest dreams. Now I cannot move at all!'

'You will, don't worry. Stay where you are for a moment.'

He snorted. 'I have no choice—even the visit to the bathroom was agony, *chica*; getting there and back nearly finished me off!'

Judith laughed unkindly, and went to her room to collect a flask of oil. She peeled off her sweater and rolled up sleeves, then tied her hair back with a ribbon and returned to the invalid, her face alight with purpose. Rafael regarded her uneasily.

'What are you going to do to me, Judith?'

'Loosen you up, that's all. First I'm going to remove your pillows. Right, that's it—now lie flat on your stomach.'

He turned over with extreme care, the duvet sliding to the floor. He wore thin white cotton pyjama trousers, and lying face down he looked suddenly vulnerable, for all his magnificent physique. Judith made herself consider him impersonally, to regard the body beneath her hands as just another patient. For the first few moments it was difficult, then automatically her trained fingers took command, moving over his oiled skin, probing the tight-locked muscles, loosening and kneading in smooth, unhurried movements. At first she could hear the occasional catch of breath as she touched some particularly sore spot, but gradually the muscular body began to relax under her touch, the tension gradually easing from his muscles. The task was not easy for Judith, not only because the bed was much lower than the surgical couch the patient normally occupied, but because, try as she might, it was impossible to forget entirely that it was Rafael who lay unresisting beneath her touch. For a while he lay lax beneath her hands, then to her surprise she could feel him tensing again. Judith frowned.

'Turn over,' she ordered. 'I'll just do a quick mobilisation——'

'No,' he burst out, and stayed where he was.

She knelt beside him. 'I won't hurt you, Rafael, I promise. I just cup your chin in one hand——'

'No!'

Judith thought she realised the problem. 'Are you afraid I'll hurt your throat?'

'Of course not—it is not my throat which troubles me, you stupid girl.' Suddenly he twisted round and pulled her on the bed beside him, staring into her startled eyes as he clamped her tightly to him. 'I may be just another arrangement of muscles and sinews to you Judith, but your hands are driving *me* insane!'

Judith stared, speechless, into his eyes, where flames literally burned as he stared into hers. He turned on one side, drawing her full length against him, and through the thick denim and thin cotton that separated them the reason for his disquiet was immediately obvious, his arousal an urgent, living presence. Her mouth dried and her eyes widened to dark, shining discs of suspense as very slowly he moved a little to free a hand sufficiently to flick each of her shirt buttons free of its mooring, pausing between each one to wait, his eyes questioning before he moved on to the next. Held in thrall by his nearness Judith said nothing at all, lying motionless as he slid the shirt from her shoulders and let it fall to the floor. Rafael's face was austere and taut, no hint of the performer now. This was the basic man in the grip of a need that some part of Judith's mind recognised as total. Against the urgency of the physical desire rising inside her any doubts or reservations were suddenly irrelevant. Nothing on earth mattered at this moment but the deep need to be loved, and to give everything of herself in return.

The mutual spell held them in breathless silence as his fingers moved caressingly over her bare shoulders, cupping them, sliding over her shoulderblades to the small clip between them to unfasten and discard the last barrier between her skin and his. Instantly their breathing quickened, shallow and uneven, a rhythm that moved Judith's breasts in soft, ravishing friction against his chest, Rafael's eyes drawn in fascination to their motion, his gaze a burn she felt on her skin. She was conscious of her nipples unfolding, erecting in response to the almost tactile caress of his eyes, but still he held her upper arms and just looked at her, his square white teeth clenched together as he ran his eyes over her body. The tension built unbearably inside Judith and suddenly he moved, pulling the ribbon from her hair and pushing her flat, his mouth a sudden, avid demand on hers. She was ready for him, a hunger in her response that sent him wild as her hands moved constantly over his back and shoulders, nothing remotely impersonal now in their touch as she gave herself up with joy to his embrace, yielding utterly in a fusion of lips and tongues and mingled breath. Breathing soon became difficult, and Rafael's mouth released hers and began to rove, following a downward path in the wake of his caressing fingers to seek her pointing nipples, his lips and tongue teasing until she writhed in gasping silence, liquid fire running through her entire body at his touch.

Judith shook her head violently in blind entreaty as his caresses stopped, but his pause was only to strip off their remaining covering until they were moulded together in full contact at last, lying motionless for a moment or two to taste the sensation before Rafael resumed his voyage of discovery. His progress was torturingly slow, a savouring of every last inch of her as his mouth and hands moved in a passionate pere-grination to the tips of her toes and back again. When at long last his mouth finally returned to hers, his kiss was different, even more urgent than before. 'Judith?' he questioned huskily, and she answered him wordlessly, arching her body to receive his.

They came together with a finality that consumed every last iota of energy in their bodies in the mutual conflagration. Afterwards they fell deeply asleep in each other's arms, lost to the world for hours, until a watery afternoon sun sent a glow into the room and Judith stirred reluctantly. Rafael's arms tightened at once, holding her still.

'*Mi amor,*' he murmured softly, and turned her face up to his for a brief, gentle kiss as ravishing in its own way as the more urgent caresses of before.

'We should get up,' suggested Judith without conviction.

'Why?'

'It must be late . . .'

'So?'

'Oh well, if you're tired——' She slid deeper under the duvet and put her parted mouth against his chest.

'I said nothing of feeling tired, *querida.*' There was a breathless, laughing note in his voice as his teeth caught in her earlobe and his fingers wound possessively in her hair.

'If we are not tired,' Judith said primly, 'we should not be in bed.'

'And what shall we do if we get up?' demanded Rafael. 'I warn you I have no intention of chopping wood.'

Judith moved a little to look up at him in concern.

'Are you still sore?'

'No. I have been cured—one way and another.' His eyes gleamed at her. 'Do not, I command, use the same method with anyone else.'

Her eyes narrowed. 'Command?'

Rafael shrugged. ' "Plead" is better?'

'Not characteristic—but better.' Judith smiled at him lazily and clasped her hands behind her head. His eyes dilated as they watched her.

'Don't,' he said huskily. 'It calls attention to that part of you which already keeps me awake at night.'

Judith dropped her arms hastily and turned her head away, suddenly absurdly shy. 'I must get up,' she said breathlessly.

'Not yet.' Rafael drew her into his arms and laid his rough cheek against hers. 'Was it good for you, *querida*?' His voice deepened to a caressing note that made her shiver involuntarily.

'You know very well it was—and for you?'

'*Un milagro*—a miracle. The most wonderful experience of my life.'

'Of which there have been many such experiences, Don Rafael!'

'I would lie if I said otherwise, alas.' He held her away from him, his eyes searching. 'Does it spoil it for you, Judith? To know there have been other women?'

'No,' she said, meeting his eyes candidly. 'I'd be a fool if it did.' She smiled impishly. 'Perhaps I should be grateful to them for contributing to your expertise!'

'*Bruja!*' He shook her hard and kissed her until Judith pushed him away and leapt out of bed clutching her clothes to her as she fled from the room. 'Come back!' he yelled, searching wildly for something to cover his nakedness.

'I'm hungry,' she called, and shut herself in her room.

Ten minutes later, bathed and dressed, they met in the kitchen and went into each other's arms as naturally as if it were a life-long habit. They heated the left-over soup together and ate it with bread and cheese and endless cups of coffee, talking and talking, the floodgates open as they explored each other's minds with as much urge to learn as their bodies had experienced earlier.

'We have more in common than I would ever have imagined,' admitted Judith at one stage, as they discovered a mutual passion for following tennis and athletics, reading spinechillers and crime novels, watching Western films, eating good food.

'And in one respect we function in most perfect accord,' said Rafael, his eyes glowing as he caressed the hand he held.

'But that isn't enough for——' Judith stopped, confused.

'A basis for a relationship?' he suggested gently.

They looked long into each other's eyes before Judith nodded slowly.

'Yes. Mutual interests last longer than sex.'

'Is that what we experienced, Judith? Just sex?' The glow died and his eyes grew sombre.

'You would know more about it than me, I grant you.' Judith looked away. How could she say that for her it had been everything any woman could ever wish for, passion and tenderness and a final savagery that had taken every part of her by storm.

'I *know* more, yes, but I am talking about feelings, little one. Was mere physical sensation the only thing you felt when we were together?' Rafael was relentless.

'No,' said Judith baldly, and got up to clear away, ignoring his triumphant smile as he allowed her to change the subject to the more mundane matter of what they should eat for dinner. When they sat over a simple meal of omelettes and salad much later that night Judith said, after some hesitation'.

'How long are you going to stay prisoner, Rafael?'

Rafael looked up from his meal, his eyes questioning.

'You mean within this house, Judith?'

'Not exactly, but it'll do for starters.'

He frowned. 'I suppose we could go out in the car if you would be willing to play chauffeur in your little Morris. I was stupid to drive down here in the Lotus—the anaesthetic must have affected my thinking powers. It simply never occurred to me that a less noticeable vehicle would be better once I was here on my own; I just followed Bryn down and have not been out since. He did all the shopping while he was here.'

'I heard, down at the Anchor.'

'Did anyone suspect I was staying with him, do you think?'

Judith shook her head, giving him a crooked little grin.

'I don't want to puncture your ego, Rafael, but I have a feeling Brynmor Tudor is much more of a celebrity in this part of the world than ever you were.'

Rafael laughed good-humouredly. 'And so he should be. He's the home-grown product, no?'

'Would you like to go out tomorrow?' persisted Judith. 'We could penetrate into deepest Dyfed, walk for a bit. It would do you good—you must be stir-crazy by this time.'

'For you—anything, *chica*. There is an old tweed hat of Bryn's on a hook in the back kitchen, and a truly disreputable jacket he wears for the fishing. I brought my own boots, and of course I shall wear the indispensable dark glasses.' Rafael leaned forward to kiss the tip of her nose, then cheerfully washed dishes while Judith made coffee, mentally warning herself sternly not to be so happy, to remember that this was just playing house, a little diversion to be taken lightly.

'You could wear the black track-suit and that terrifying ski-helmet thing of yours,' she suggested with a sly grin. 'You'd probably scare half the local populace to death, but at least no one would know who was doing it!'

He laughed uproariously and seized her round the waist, kissing her hard. 'Come,' he said imperiously. 'We will play backgammon again, and tonight the victor chooses the prize.'

Judith failed to win a single game, and had to admit defeat after only two.

'Infuriating,' she said crossly, and eyed her glass of brandy with hostility. 'I'll remember to avoid alcohol in future—it doesn't improve my game. Either that or you were cheating!'

Rafael turned eyes of limpid innocence on her and laid a hand on his heart. 'How could you even think such a thing, *querida*!'

'H'm.' Judith was unconvinced. 'And what prize had you in mind, anyway?'

'Since you accuse me of cheating,' he said with arrogance, 'I shall not trouble to claim one.'

Judith stared at him blankly as he put the backgammon set away, gave her a graceful bow and bade her good night with formality. She watched him leave the room with a hint of swagger, feeling forlorn as

she collected their glasses and took them to the kitchen.
She could hardly believe that Rafael had actually taken
himself off in a huff over such a little thing. When she
went upstairs she looked at his door for a moment, then
passed by with her chin lifted. To hell with him. In her
room she cleansed her face with a vigour that left it
glowing, and brushed her hair until it crackled and
sparked like an extension of her bad temper. She pulled
on her nightgown and was just turning down the bed
when she saw the door opening slowly. Deciding it was
probably one of those errant draughts Rafael had
talked about she went irritably to close it, nearly dying
of fright at the apparition in the hall, all in black and
with the all too familiar mask. Judith screamed and
banged the door shut in sharp, instinctive terror, her
fright turning to unadultered fury as Rafael charged
through the doorway, tearing off the helmet in
consternation as she turned on him like an avenging
angel.

'Never, never, never do that again, you—you . . .'
Almost beside herself with rage she pummelled his
broad chest, breathless with the desire to lash out at
him.

'Judith, *mi amor*! I am sorry, sorry. Forgive me,
please. It was a joke—I thought you would laugh.' With
an effort Rafael caught her flailing fists and held her
fast, his powerful arms holding her still, frustrating her
savage efforts to be free. To her horror Judith began to
cry and Rafael became utterly frantic. 'Please! Judith,
querida, do not weep, I implore you, hush, little one, *mi
amor*, *mi corazón* . . .' He cradled her to his chest,
lapsing into a stream of liquid Spanish intended to
soothe and comfort. After a while she calmed down,
leaning limply against him.

'I thought it was you when I was attacked,' she said
hoarsely at last, 'that's why I was taken by surprise. I
really thought it was you, but it was *him*——'

Rafael took in a deep shuddering breath. 'What
can I say, Judith? I grovel at your feet—see!' In one
fluid, graceful movement Rafael went down on his
knees, face turned up to hers in passionate sup-

plication, and in spite of herself Judith's tears turned to laughter.

'God, you're impossible—get up you melodramatic idiot. Which role are you playing now, may I enquire?'

He leapt to his feet and stood staring down at her, a look in his eyes she recognised with sudden excitement. The smooth silk of her nightgown was suddenly restricting across her breasts, and her lips parted, the tears dried by the heat of her cheeks.

'I assure you I'm not playing, Judith.' Rafael's voice was rougher, deeper as he reached out a hand and touched her lower lip with a long forefinger. Instinctively her teeth closed gently on his fingertip and his eyes dilated. The naked question in them quickened her already hammering pulse. 'I want my prize now, *querida.*'

'Even though you cheated?' she said unsteadily.

'I would do far worse to achieve my desire, *mi amor*—and *you* are my desire. You know only too well it has been so from our first meeting.' Rafael drew her slowly into his arms, running a loving hand down her spine, suddenly jerking her hips hard against him, his other hand sliding into her hair to bring her parted mouth to his. Judith's knees gave and she melted against him pliantly, yielding to his mouth and hands so completely that almost without knowing how they got there they were together in the wide double bed in a breathless, hot excited world of their own, with no thoughts of past or future allowed to intrude into the wonder that was now.

During the days that followed they tramped the remote green hills beyond Morfa by day, returning to evenings by the fire and long, rapturous nights in the big bed, occupying a dream world of their own, an enchanted time unlike any experience in Judith's existence before. The few people encountered on their walks took little interest in them beyond a polite greeting, and Judith did any shopping necessary alone in Cardigan, hurrying through the chore as rapidly as possible, grudging every second she spent apart from Rafael. A couple of guarded telephone calls to Honor to assure her all was well, and a postcard of Morfa beach sent to her father and mother were all the communication Judith made with the outside world.

One evening, Rafael joined her on the hearthrug, kissing her mouth with a lingering tenderness. 'I am deeply conscious of my debt to you, *querida*,' he muttered against her skin.

'Don't talk of debts, Rafael.' Judith's dark eyes were luminous as she looked into his. 'You have no obligation to me of any kind. I came because I was very worried about you, and I stayed because you wanted me to, and because I wanted to just as much. I had no idea that things would—would happen the way they have, I'll admit.'

'Do you regret this?'

'How could I? These past few days have been idyllic; the happiest of my life.'

Rafael sat straight, putting her a little away from him so he could face her, his voice suddenly urgent.

'Then marry me, Judith!'

She sat motionless, her dark eyes wide with shock.

'*Marry* you, Rafael! But—but——'

'But what?' There was stormy entreaty in his look. 'You do not care enough for me? I am too old? I cannot sing any more I know——'

'Stop, stop,' she implored. 'I don't care a button whether you can sing or not. And you know only too well that I care. I couldn't, I mean I wouldn't—oh stop looking at me like that, Rafael. God knows if this is how you make love at your advanced stage of decrepitude I think it's just as well I didn't know you when you were a young stud—Rafael!'

The rest of her protest was lost against his mouth as he hauled her across his knees and kissed her until she moaned for mercy.

'Then say yes,' he muttered, his mouth roaming over her face, his teeth nibbling delicately at her earlobe. 'A small word, *chica*. Very easy to say, no? Say it, say it!'

Judith pushed him away with a superhuman effort, shaking back her tangled hair.

'Now steady on a bit, Rafael.' She held him off as he

would have pulled her close again. 'No, please. I can't think rationally when you touch me. And I'd like to clarify a few points.'

Rafael sat upright, folding his arms across his chest.

'See, I am good. Now what is it that troubles you?'

'When you talk of marriage,' Judith began hesitantly, 'just what precisely do you mean?'

He frowned at her, his brows drawn together in surprise.

'It means something different in this country from mine? You and me, Judith. Together for life. A home, children if we are fortunate. The normal things anyone expects from marriage, no?'

'Where would we live? Your house in Spain?'

'If you wish. Or anywhere else you like——'

'And I would have to give up my job?'

'That, definitely.' His face darkened. 'I do not enjoy the thought of you touching other men, however old they are, or ill. This must stop.'

Judith's full mouth took on rather a set look.

'I see. And what will you do, Rafael? If you can't sing any more how do you propose to fill your life?'

He shrugged. 'Grow olives, write my autobiography, play with my children, make love with you. An idyll, no?'

'No,' said Judith positively.

They stared at each other for a moment.

'You mean that?' he demanded harshly.

She nodded. 'Think about it, Rafael——'

'Do you think I have not?' he retorted bitterly. 'Since I have been certain my voice would never be the same I have done little else but think. I was almost crazy from thinking by the time you arrived.'

'Then how can you even imagine that the life you mapped out could ever be enough for you—or me?' Judith put out a hand imploringly. 'You're accustomed to a frantically busy, demanding public life, and I'm used to quite a demanding job myself. Neither of us cares very much for inactivity. So how could we go off and live some idle, lotus-eating existence in your castle in Spain with any possible hope of being happy?'

'To be with you is happiness enough, Judith.' He stared sombrely into the dying fire.

'Thank you. At this moment I feel the same about you—but would that last? You might get bored with me. I don't have any music in my make-up at all, whereas for you it's been your whole life. Once the first heat of sexual attraction dies down a bit would there be enough common interest left to hold us together?'

Rafael rose slowly to his feet and stood looking down at her, his eyes dull and lifeless. 'If you have need to ask yourself such a question, Judith, it is unnecessary for me to answer. For yourself you know already.'

Judith hugged her knees in silence, looking up at him with troubled eyes. God, how she longed to throw herself into his arms, let the rest of the world go hang, ride off into the sunset and the world of happy ever after. But it was all too soon, too sudden. There was no insurance it would last, that her unadulterated company would be enough to satisfy this gifted, cultured man for life.

'Rafael,' she faltered, 'I . . .'

'Say nothing, Judith. I understand. I was presuming too much. Let us forget my—my proposal, turn back the clock to an hour ago.' Rafael knelt to rake the embers of the fire and turned to look at her. 'Shall I put another log on the fire, or shall we let it die out?'

The question sounded ominously symbolic. Judith managed a shaky smile and got up.

'It's late. Perhaps we should be going to bed.'

In silence they turned out the lights and climbed the stairs together, tension mounting in Judith as they reached the landing. Rafael hesitated a moment, then bent and kissed her forehead gently.

'Good night, Judith. Sleep well.'

'Good night.' Like an automaton she turned away to walk to her room, her back proudly straight, iron control keeping the tears at bay as she closed the curtains and undressed. It was only when she turned on the taps in the bathroom that she gave way, the sound of the water drowning her sobs as she wept like a lost child. For most of the night she lay with her head buried in the pillows, sobs shaking her spasmodically until from sheer weariness she finally dozed, only to wake again to the sound of throbbing outside. Stumbling hastily from bed she peered through a crack in the curtains, just able to make out the low, dark outline of the Lotus in the drive, its engine running as Rafael opened the gate. He drove the car through, returned to shut the gate, then drove off, the car disappearing down the lane out of sight—and out of her life, she thought drearily.

There seemed no point in returning to bed. Judith dressed, packed her case, tidied the room and stripped the bed. With a sigh she took the bedlinen downstairs and loaded it into the washing machine. As she was making herself some tea she caught sight of the envelope propped against the percolator and opened it with shaking fingers. The note inside was brief.

'*Querida*,' it began, 'it seems best to steal away in the night like a coward. Forgive me. If I had tried to say goodbye I would not have found the strength to leave you. And leave you it seems I must. I had no right to ask you to share my life now that it has no aim or purpose. My gratitude to you, Judith, for seeking me out and bringing me to what senses I possess. The memory of the lovely days, and nights, we spent together will remain in my heart forever. *Adiós*. Rafael.'

Judith stared at the note, her mouth trembling. Typical, she told herself angrily. Flowery, sentimental, mawkish, like one of his precious librettos; with each insult she tore the paper into smaller pieces and took them outside to hurl them in the dustbin, brushing her hands together afterwards. She paused for a moment to take in a gulp of fresh, cool air then went inside to make an attack on the house. She hung out the clean sheets on the line in the garden, careless of being seen now—there was no longer any point in hiding; no one was likely to be interested in *her*. Judith relaid the sitting-room fire, polished, vacuumed, swept and scrubbed until her hands were sore and her back ached in competition with her heart. She dismissed the latter fiercely, dinning into herself the fact that she had no

cause for complaint—she had been the one who turned
Rafael down, not the other way around.

But as she ironed duvet covers and sheets Judith
faced the fact that troubled her most. It had never
occurred to her that Rafael would simply remove
himself, with never a word as to his destination, nor any
hint of what he had in mind for the future; the most
obvious place for him to make for was probably
Granada, and Judith sighed bleakly, wondering if she
had been right to refuse his unexpected proposal. She
could have been on her way there with him now—no,
she couldn't. The practical side of her remembered it
was necessary to give in her notice at Hardwick
Memorial if she decided to leave, and there was Honor,
not to mention her parents, to consider, and in any case
there was no use repining. The whole thing was
academic now. She must put Rafael out of her mind,
starting right now.

Judith rang Honor and told her she would be in
Hardwick much later that night, warning her sister not
to wait up, then locked up the immaculate house,
posted the keys through the letterbox and drove the
Morris away from Morfa as fast as the elderly little car
would allow. Her next holiday would be spent
somewhere like Morocco or Iceland, or anywhere as
different as possible from the solid house inside its
secret grey walls, high above Cardigan Bay.

It was past midnight when Judith reached Hardwick
and locked the Morris up in the coach house. Wearily
she carried her case and collection of carrier bags down
the lane to Chantry Cottage, glad to see a light showing
in the sitting-room window. Honor must have waited
up for her after all. While she was trying to free a hand
to put her key in the lock the door opened, the light
from the hall outlining two figures instead of one. For
one blinding moment of joy she thought the man with
Honor was Rafael, then Honor drew her inside and
fussed over her, and she could see that it was only
Martin.

Only Martin! Judith looked at Honor closely when
all the greetings were over and her sister pushed her

into the sitting-room. Honor wore a look of suppressed
excitement and Martin had quite visibly lost the rather
distant look he normally wore.

'Is there something I should know?' asked Judith,
smiling.

Martin put his arm around Honor. 'I hope you'll be
as happy as I am that your sister has consented to
marry me,' he said proudly. 'Though I'm not sure that's
possible. I must be the happiest chap in the world
tonight.'

Judith seized Honor and kissed her fondly, then
kissed Martin in turn.

'About time, too,' she said bluntly.

Honor laughed, blushing. 'Now then, Judith. Don't
embarrass me, please—you'll have Martin believing I've
been pursuing him. Let me get you something to
eat——'

'Just a sandwich, or something, love. I'm not very
hungry.'

Honor looked at her sharply. 'You must have
something, Judith, after that long drive; you look worn
out. I wasn't expecting you back for another day or two
actually.'

'No. Things altered, so I came home.' Judith's face
was white with fatigue and Honor said no more,
hurrying off to make a snack.

'How did you like Morfa?' asked Martin when he
and Judith were alone.

'Lovely little place—it must be beautiful when the
weather's warmer. It turned blustery and a bit cold,
unfortunately.'

Martin was too well bred to probe any further and
followed Judith's lead when she reverted to the subject
of the engagement. He was only too happy to talk
about Honor anyway, surprising Judith with the news
that the wedding was to be as soon as it could be
arranged without resorting to a special licence, adding
that her parents seemed very pleased by the news.

'Pleased!' exclaimed Judith. 'I bet Mother's feet
haven't touched the ground since she heard.'

Martin grinned. 'Aunt Lavinia's rather chuffed, too.

By the way Honor and I are going down to Abergavenny this weekend—would you care to come with us?'

'Lord, no! I mean, it's really very sweet of you, but no thanks. I need some time to relax before going back to the hospital.' Judith yawned wearily.

Honor appeared with a tray, casting a sharp look at Judith.

'You look worn out. Eat these sandwiches, and I'll pour coffee.'

'Shouldn't it be champagne?'

'We've already had some with Miss Gresham at a celebratory dinner,' said Honor happily. 'I wish you'd come home sooner; you could have joined us.'

And toasted absent friends, thought Judith dully, then blinked and smiled brightly at Honor. 'You kept very quiet about all this when I telephoned.'

'It hadn't happened then.' Honor and Martin exchanged mutual looks of pure happiness, and a spearthrust of envy pierced Judith. She abandoned the sandwiches half eaten.

'Sorry, love, I had a snack on the way back,' she lied. 'But I'd love more coffee.'

Honor refilled her cup, then said bluntly,

'Right then, Judith. We've observed all the preliminaries, and we already know you found Rafael. So tell us what happened.'

'But only if you really want to,' said Martin gently.

Judith smiled wearily and gave them the barest outline of the time spent at the cottage, omitting any mention of how fast and far the relationship between Rafael and herself had progressed, and glossing over the real reason for his departure.

'He was much better by the time he left,' she wound up, 'which was gratifying. He was a bit low when I first arrived.'

Martin was deeply affected by the news that the glorious voice was never to be heard again except on recordings.

'God what a tragedy! Poor old Raf. I was afraid of something like this, of course, but one keeps on hoping for the best.' He looked at Judith unhappily. 'Has he decided what he's going to do—where was he headed for when he left?'

'He wasn't sure; Granada, possibly,' she said vaguely. 'I don't think he'd made up his mind about how he was going to occupy himself.'

'Are you going to see him again?' asked Honor quietly.

'No. I'm not.' Suddenly Judith could take no more and jumped to her feet, her eyes overbright. 'I'm just going to have to love you and leave you, my dears, I'm dead on my feet. Good night, and congratulations again. I'm so very pleased, it couldn't have happened to two nicer people.'

'See you in the morning, love,' said Honor quickly, aware that her young sister had reached the end of her tether. 'Sleep well.'

Fat chance of that, thought Judith miserably as she hefted her suitcase up the stairs. Tired out though she was it was far more likely the night would be spent in cursing herself for being stupid enough to turn Rafael down. And she was right.

CHAPTER TEN

IT was afternoon before Judith saw Honor next day. Her sister had spent the morning at the library, and came home at lunchtime with one of the daily tabloids in her hand. Her face was troubled as she handed it to Judith.

'I confiscated it,' she said. 'I thought you ought to see it. Look at page five.'

Judith's eyes widened as she saw a blurred picture of herself hanging out washing in the garden of Brynmorfa. The photographer had only managed a back view, and the long, blowing hair and dark jeans could have belonged to any tall, long-legged girl, but the photograph was a shock just the same. 'Mystery girl in Welsh lovenest,' ran the caption. 'Rumour has it that super-warbler Rafael David has been recuperating at the Welsh hideout of fellow singer Brynmor Tudor. Always a favourite of the ladies, Rafael's convalescence has been helped along by the anonymous lovely above. A Welsh au pair?' There was more, but Judith threw the paper down in disgust.

'How did he manage that shot, I wonder! Must have been the zoom lens to end all zoom lenses. Ugh!'

Honor's expression was deeply compassionate as she put an arm round Judith.

'Things go wrong, darling?'

Judith gave her a sad little smile. 'Things went very right for a while, but it's entirely my fault they turned sour again, not Rafael's. And now he's vanished and I don't know where he is, and I'm back to square one again. Only this time it's ten times worse, Honor.'

'Why?'

'Because I rather think I've made the biggest mistake of my life, and I have no one to blame but myself.' Judith had no tears left. She leaned against Honor dry-eyed. 'Sorry, love, I'm spoiling all your glow. Let's forget about me—it's over and done with. So tell me when the wedding is.'

Although yearning to give comfort Honor was wise enough to realise there was nothing she could say or do to help, and followed Judith's lead, plunging into wedding arrangements as a diversion.

'You'll be wanting to sell Chantry Cottage, too,' said Judith practically. 'Don't worry about me, Honor, I'll soon find digs somewhere else.'

'Martin suggested you move into Gresham House with us, but I couldn't see that appealing to you, somehow.'

'How right you are. Intrude on two newly-weds!' Judith grinned cheekily. 'I'll share a flat with someone, or . . .'

'You don't have to. I won't sell the cottage until— well, not for the time being, anyway. You can pay me rent if you like—even have someone to go halves, only preferably female or Mrs Dean will never stand the excitement!'

'Are you sure, Honor? Don't you need the money? I'd like that better than anything, of course, but I hope you're not doing it just for me.'

'Martin's well off, which is common knowledge, so I'm not likely to want for pin-money.' She gave Judith a hug. 'Besides, I'd like to think of you here for a bit, at least until you've, well——'

'Got my act together a bit better,' said Judith ruefully. 'Thank you, big sister, I appreciate it very much.'

Judith was to be maid of honour at the wedding, which was to be very quiet and to take place at the church near the Russells' home. Kate Russell came to stay with the two girls beforehand and went on a mad whirl of spending, buying a spectacular plumed hat for the occasion.

'I must have something to impress the neighbours,' she stated, examining herself in the hat when they got back to the cottage. 'Because I write thrillers people expect me to be eccentric.'

'You *are* eccentric,' said Judith promptly.

'Nonsense. Outspoken perhaps. Which is more than can be said for you, my cherub; you haven't said a word about your holiday in Wales.'

'It was very quiet,' said Judith, avoiding Honor's anguished eye. 'Not a tremendous amount to do in a place like Morfa.'

'Then why go there?' demanded her mother.

'Martin suggested it,' said Honor cleverly, which silenced Mrs Russell very effectively. Martin could do no wrong.

Just the same Judith wished she never had gone to Morfa as the time before the wedding dragged slowly past. Thoughts of Rafael haunted her, making life a torment it was difficult to conceal. Never a sufferer from insomnia previously Judith took to playing squash every evening on top of a full day's work with the idea of getting to bed so exhausted sleep would blot out her melancholy for a brief respite. With determination she immersed herself in her job, threw herself into the wedding plans, but without much success. Honor, loving and sensitive as always, was troubled.

'You're wearing yourself to a frazzle, Judith,' she said at last. 'To be blunt you'll look like nothing on earth at the wedding if you carry on like this.'

'The spectre at the feast, you mean?' Judith grinned remorsefully, and yawned. 'I'm sorry, Honor. I know I'm being a pain—but I promise I'll get it out of my system before the big day.'

Honor hesitated, then came out with what was worrying her. 'I know you prefer to keep off the subject, darling, but just how deeply did you get involved with Rafael?'

Judith looked her sister straight in the eye. 'If you mean did we sleep together, yes, we did, though that's a ridiculous euphemism really. It has nothing to do with what actually happens in bed between a man and woman before they actually sleep—if and when they do.' She smiled in apology as Honor's cheeks went bright pink. 'Sorry—I didn't mean to shock you, just make it clear that I don't regret anything. I'd do it all over again, even knowing how it would end. We had a perfect few days together. I'll remember them for the rest of my life.' She smiled bleakly. 'Just listen to me! I sound like one of Rafael's operatic heroines—it must have rubbed off.'

Honor sighed. 'I was so afraid you'd get hurt, Judith.'

'And I did. But it was worth it. One can't always choose the soft option.' Judith squeezed Honor's hand. 'I'm sorry. I really will try to be better from now on, I promise. You're the bride, and I don't want to spoil anything for you. I'll be fine, you'll see.'

It was one thing to make verbal promises. Carrying them out was another matter. Judith found the constant wedding talk almost unbearable at times, agonisingly aware that she could have been arranging her own if she had been less chicken-hearted. It no longer mattered what Rafael wanted to do with his life. As the days passed Judith knew with more and more certainty that wherever Rafael was and whatever he was doing she wanted to be with him, sharing that life for better, for worse, in sickness and in health, for ever and ever, amen. Determined that neither Honor nor anyone else should suspect the depth of her unhappiness, Judith spent the whole of one sleepless night sorting herself out. The blame for her misery lay squarely at her own door, and there was no way of finding Rafael this time, however much she wanted to put things right between them. And even if she could there was enough of the hidalgo in Rafael's make-up to make it fairly certain he would hardly take kindly to rejection, of any kind. In short, she had made her own bed, and now she had no choice but to lie in it. Alone.

From that night on Judith threw herself whole-heartedly into preparations for the wedding, determined to block Rafael from her mind. She went with Honor to choose her wedding dress, and at the same time found just the thing she wanted herself, a demure little brown suit with swinging pleated skirt and brass-buttoned collarless jacket, plus a wildly expensive beige silk shirt with an outsize velvet bow under its white collar. She even bought a dashing, trilby-style brown velvet hat to wear low over her eyes, though hats were normally not an item in her wardrobe. It was only when she and Honor were actually in the car on their way to Abergavenny two days before the wedding that Judith thought to ask who was acting as best man.

'An old friend of Martin's from Army days,' said Honor, and Judith relaxed. No Rafael, that was obvious.

Quiet wedding or not, the household in Abergavenny was in a fair state of prenuptial excitement when they arrived. Gwyneth, the true-red Welsh Nationalist daily, was positively ecstatic because Honor was marrying into a 'posh family'.

'And what about you?' she asked Judith bluntly. 'You've got a bit of catching up to do, my girl. Here's Honor getting married for the second time and you haven't even managed it once yet.'

'Neither have you,' retorted Judith, grinning, 'so don't go picking on me.'

Gwyneth tossed her tightly-permed grey curls and picked up a hammer.

'Not for the want of asking, don't you worry, but I never fancied it myself.'

Mrs Russell eyed the hammer with hostility.

'And just what do you intend doing with that, Gwyneth?'

'I'll just knock a nail in that loosepiece of trellis in the garden—don't want it collapsing on the guests, now, do you?'

Honor and Judith giggled as Gwyneth's stout, bustling figure disappeared past the kitchen window on her quest. Mrs Russell scowled.

'Your father's already out there fixing the wretched thing. I don't know why she has this bee in her bonnet that he can't be trusted to do anything manual.' She sighed in exasperation. 'If only I could persuade Gwyneth to confine herself to the housework.'

'Oh Mother, she's lovely,' protested Honor with a chuckle. 'Besides she does keep the house spick and span too.'

'Oh I'll grant you that,' allowed Kate, 'especially where soap and water are involved—I swear there's something sensual to Gwyneth about a scrubbing brush and hot suds. Now, tell me when Martin's arriving.'

'Not until the actual ceremony. He and Miss Gresham are staying with an old friend of hers in Chepstow overnight and coming on from there in the morning.' Honor smiled radiantly. 'He says he won't risk seeing me beforehand because of bad luck and all that. We're to abide by the rules.'

'You always do,' said Judith, giving her a hug. 'You and Martin make a perfect pair.'

'Of course they do,' said Kate, then broke off, her face appalled. 'Merciful heaven, what has your father done to himself *now*?'

Dan Russell came in with a finger streaming with blood, his face sheepish.

'Gwyneth's hammer slipped—is there a plaster in the house?'

*   *   *

No further incidents marred the wedding preparations and Honor's big day dawned bright and crisp. The Russells made the short journey to the village in a hired Rolls Royce, and when Kate left the others to take her place inside the small church as the familiar strains of the organ heralded the arrival of the bride, Dan Russell offered his arm to his elder daughter, and Honor, in ivory wool dress and tiny velvet hat frothing with marabou, walked proudly with him down the aisle to meet her groom. Judith followed behind, the sudden change from bright sunlight to candle-lit dimness blinding her momentarily to anything but her father's grey-clad back and Honor's fluttering feathers. Then Martin turned with a tender smile to greet his bride and Judith saw with shock that the man standing beside him, tall and remote in formal grey morning coat, was Rafael. For a long, charged moment their eyes locked together, then Rafael turned to face the altar with Martin, leaving Judith like a statue, staring sightlessly in front of her, hearing nothing of the service, or her mother's frankly audible sniffs behind her. She recovered with a start as Honor and Martin moved up to the altar with the vicar, realising the main part of the ceremony was over. Aware in every fibre of the tall, elegant figure standing so near, Judith felt a sudden hot stab of anger at being kept in the dark, dismissing it at once as she assumed Honor must have thought it would be easier for her this way. She cast a brief, hungry look at Rafael's sombre profile, then kept her eyes averted until everyone was called into the vestry for the ritual of kisses and congratulations over the signing of the register.

Kate Russell was madly impressed to find Martin's 'old friend' was Rafael David, and her frank delight in meeting him entirely glossed over any constraint as he and Judith greeted each other. Conscious of the appeal on Honor's face Judith gave Rafael her hand, her heart missing a beat at the touch of his fingers.

'How are you, Judith?' he asked softly, under cover of the buzz of conversation going on around them.

'All right,' she said woodenly. 'And you?'

'No. I am not.' Rafael's eyes burned at her for an instant before he turned away to speak to Judith's father. She took in a shaky breath and encountered the shrewd face of Miss Gresham.

'Judith, my dear, do I find you well?' There was sympathy in her kind eyes.

Judith smiled valiantly. 'Fine, Miss Gresham. Isn't it a lovely day?'

'A very happy occasion, I'm more pleased than I can say that Honor is now one of the family—I've never seen Martin so relaxed and, well—joyful is the word, I think.'

'Honor too. They're good for each other.' Judith went on chatting brightly, hardly aware of what she was saying, glad when her father shepherded them both from the vestry to follow the others from the church for a brief photographic session outside before driving back to the Russell home, where a firm of local caterers was providing the wedding breakfast.

Judith hardly knew whether to be sorry or glad when she and Rafael were seated next to each other at the big round table in the dining-room, and with a murmur of apology removed her hat before they began the meal, her head aching with tension.

'That is much better,' said Rafael gravely. 'Now I can see your beautiful face.'

By no means sure this was a good thing Judith cast a hunted glance about her, but her father was engrossed in conversation with Miss Gresham on one hand, and across from her Kate Russell was simultaneously engaged in conversation with her new son-in-law and keeping an eagle eye on the caterers. Judith relaxed a fraction.

'How is your throat, Rafael?' she asked quietly.

'My throat is well, my body is well. All I lack is a voice and a heart.' He spoke in such a quiet, conversational monotone Judith looked at him startled before nodding dazedly at the waiter offering her champagne.

'Don't——' she began painfully as the waiter moved away.

Rafael gave her a piercing, topaz look. 'Why not? I speak the truth.' He immediately turned his attention to Honor and Judith swallowed some champagne compulsively, stiffening as she met her mother's arrested look across the table. Her heart sank. The damage was done, however. Kate's mind was not the type to need more than a hint, as Judith knew only too well.

Food appeared, and Judith ate smoked salmon and roast pheasant, drank more champagne, joined in the toasts and even conducted some kind of polite conversation with Rafael. What they said was unimportant anyway. Beneath the light, conventional phrases lay another conversation entirely, and Judith hoped desperately that no one was aware of it but herself. One imploring little smile from Honor was at once guilty and triumphant, and Judith smiled back in bright reassurance, renewing her efforts at playing the part of happy wedding guest. After the meal Rafael rose to his feet and made a fluent, charming speech in toast to the bridal pair, which was answered rather more diffidently by Martin, who was obviously so happy as he sat down to clasp Honor's hand again that Mrs Russell frankly wiped away a tear, and even Miss Gresham had to resort to a handkerchief. The lump in Judith's throat was so pronounced by this stage that conversation of any kind was becoming an impossibility, and she was grateful when it was time to slip away with Honor to help her change into her travelling clothes.

'Are you angry, Judith?' said Honor immediately as Judith unzipped her.

'No, not angry. A bit shattered, I suppose, I—I don't know what I am, really.' Judith handed over the skirt of Honor's new suit and took the blouse from its hanger.

'Miss Gresham said we should have warned you, but I thought it might have spoiled everything for you.'

'Cuckoo! It's *your* wedding, not mine.' Judith managed quite a creditable laugh. 'It certainly livened things up even more for Mother. She was elated enough at having Martin for a son-in-law, but to have Rafael at the wedding really was the icing on the cake.'

Honor slid into her jacket and looked at Judith very closely. 'Do you love him, Judith?'

Judith nodded dumbly.

'Then let him know! Why waste time, like me? I've had eight years alone since Simon died and I've known Martin for nearly six of them. We could have been married long since if we had only been less inhibited about showing our feelings. If you want Rafael, grab him,' advised Honor, with surprising bluntness.

Judith laughed and kissed her sister's cheek.

'Perhaps he doesn't want to be grabbed—not by me, anyway.'

'Rubbish,' said Honor with energy. 'You can take it from me that he does.'

Soon afterwards the bride and groom went off in a flurry of good wishes, and the others turned back into the house with the inescapable feeling of anticlimax which follows the departure of bride and groom. The Russells had asked Miss Gresham to stay for the evening, promising to return her to her friend in Chepstow afterwards.

'And you, Mr David,' said Mrs Russell, smiling. 'Can we persuade you to stay too?'

Rafael gave her one of his devastating smiles in response. 'Alas,' he said regretfully, 'I cannot. I must leave very shortly for an appointment.'

Judith's spirits plummeted. Sick inside with disappointment she joined the others in regrets and offers of further refreshments before he left, but Rafael declined gracefully, thanking the Russells for their hospitality and kissing Miss Gresham goodbye. He turned to Judith and said casually,

'Perhaps you would walk with me to the car and advise me on what to provide as wedding present for your sister. I have not had an opportunity to choose anything as yet.'

'Of course,' murmured Judith politely, and in response to his hand under her elbow, walked down the drive with him after his final goodbyes were said to the others. They were silent until they reached the Lotus which was parked a little way along the lane leading to the house. Judith looked at the car in surprise.

'How did that get there?'

'I drove to the church straight from London to meet up with Martin. One of the mechanics in the village garage brought it up here while we were in church.' He turned to face her. 'When do you go back to Hardwick?'

Judith stared at him, dazed. 'What? Oh, in the morning.'

'You are driving Honor's car?'

'Yes.'

'Then take great care, Judith.' He stood for a moment longer, a brooding expression in his eyes. 'You look tired.'

'Weddings are tiring,' she said, shrugging.

He raised a hand towards her, then dropped it.

'Goodbye, Judith.'

'Goodbye,' she said forlornly, her eyes following him as without another word he unlocked the car and slid inside. The engine purred to life and with a grave salute he drove away down the narrow lane, leaving her staring blankly after him, hardly able to credit that he was gone without saying something, anything, to heal the breach between them. You made it, she reminded herself bitterly, so now you're stuck with it. Honor's instruction to grab him hadn't been so easy, after all. It was hardly possible to see Rafael now as the man who'd gasped and groaned beneath her searching hands . . . With a quick intake of breath Judith turned on her heel and walked back to the house, her eyes blank when her mother asked what gift she had suggested. Judith improvised wildly.

'I gave him a choice—anything from bath towels to a new stereo system,' she lied, and excused herself to change and give herself some time alone. What had been his motive in talking to her alone, she wondered. Nothing had been said. Judith lay on her bed for a while, just trying to get herself together again after the shock of seeing Rafael. He had looked tired too, she thought, his face thinner, the shadows darker beneath his eyes. Not that any of it had detracted in the slightest from his sheer physical impact, which had quite devastated Kate Russell, as Judith discovered when good manners finally sent her back to join the others.

'I've seen him on the television, of course,' her mother was saying, 'but it's nothing like seeing him in the flesh.'

Which was the truth, as Judith was in a position to know better than most.

'Shall I make some tea, Mother?' she asked quickly, preferring occupation to sitting around discussing Rafael's personal magnetism.

'I'll do that,' said Mr Russell quickly. 'You sit here, darling, you look tired.'

And so say all of us, thought Judith. She must look like nothing on earth if the opinion was so unanimous, and she met a sympathetic gleam in Miss Gresham's eyes as she sat down again.

'Working you hard at the hospital, Judith?' she asked kindly.

'Much the same as usual. I enjoy it—well, mostly anyway.' Judith avoided her mother's bright, astute look, and turned the conversation to the future of the newlyweds, even insinuating a thought about possible grandchildren, which was an inspired move, as both ladies found the subject fascinating in the extreme, allowing Judith to sit back and drink the tea her father brought in without having to contribute more than an occasional remark here and there.

Judith was unable to escape the inevitable inquisition, however. The moment Dan Russell drove off to Chepstow with Miss Gresham Kate fixed her daughter with a relentless eye.

'Are you in love with Rafael David, Judith?'

For a moment Judith toyed with the idea of denying it, but decided against it. Her mother would ferret the truth out in the end.

'Yes, Mother, I'm afraid I am. Me and countless other members of my sex, I imagine, so don't go making mountains out of molehills.'

Kate Russell put out a hand to touch her daughter's flushed cheek.

'Are you unhappy, darling?'

Judith nodded.

'But I'll get over it in time. It hasn't happened before for me—I'm a bit late with my first real crush, aren't I?' She smiled valiantly and began to take the pins from her upswept hair. 'What you might call a late developer—romantically anyway. Pity I chose such a remote target for my girlish devotion, isn't it?'

'Is it true that he can't sing any more?' asked Mrs Russell.

'Yes. He says he's going to grow olives and—and write his memoirs,' said Judith, omitting the rest of Rafael's plans. 'Rather an adjustment for a man of his talent to make, isn't it?'

'Cruel, poor man. He's so marvellously attractive, too—but then I don't have to rub it in, do I? Judith—am I mistaken, or did I sense some kind of response in him, too?'

'I should think he responds to most reasonably attractive women, don't you?' said Judith evasively, and yawned. 'I must get some sleep if I'm to drive back tomorrow.'

'Have lunch first this time.'

'Yes, all right.'

'Judith?'

'Yes, Mother?'

'If it's any consolation, you really are much more than reasonably attractive.' Kate met her daughter's surprised look with a whimsical smile. 'In fact you looked ravishing today.'

'Why, Mother——' Touched, Judith kissed her mother's cheek. 'Of course, you could be prejudiced. What was it you used to say? "A toad is lovely in a duckling's eye".'

'How frightfully homespun! Are you sure I said that?'

'I don't know anyone else who comes out with little gems like that, I assure you!'

Living alone at Chantry Cottage took some getting used to at first. For days after the wedding Judith was taut with a feeling of expectancy each evening after her return from the hospital. Her brain scoffed and told her Rafael had no intention of making contact, but her heart refused to listen and went on hoping, a hope that lessened as each day passed without a word. Finally the last flicker died and grimly Judith shut Rafael from her mind, her heart, from her entire life, along with the music he stood for, accepting finally that whatever they had once had together was over.

When Honor and Martin returned from their honeymoon, tanned and blissfully happy, things livened up somewhat for Judith. Martin was always involved in various activities in the town, with their related social engagements, and made a point of including Judith in many of the invitations he and Honor received. Judith was very appreciative and sometimes accepted, sometimes refused, with no wish to intrude too much on the newlyweds, whose happiness was a little painful to witness now and then, contrasting only too vividly with the emptiness of her own life, however much she tried to fill it.

Sensitive to the unhappiness behind Judith's bravely smiling face Honor often came round to the cottage in the evenings on her own when Martin was occupied at some exclusively male function. One evening she was chatting with Judith over coffee when she suddenly looked up very squarely over her cup.

'And how *are* things with you, little sister? Truthfully, I mean.'

Caught off-guard, Judith smiled ruefully. 'All right. Mostly, anyway.'

'Do you find it lonely here in the cottage? Would you prefer to live somewhere else?' Honor's eyes were searching.

'No—really. I love it here. Living alone has its compensations,' said Judith cheerfully. 'I can mooch around in a dressing gown if I want, watch all the lowbrow stuff on television you don't like, and——and——'

'Brood?'

'No. I don't brood. Not any more.'

Honor looked unconvinced.

'Have you forgotten Rafael, then?' she asked bluntly.

Judith gave her a crooked little smile. 'I wouldn't go so far as to say that, sister dear,' she said lightly. 'Not the type of person one forgets easily, is he? Let's say I've learned to live with not forgetting him.'

'Are you still in love with him?

'I'm afraid so. Seems to be a difficult habit to break now I've begun—but I'm working on it.' Judith got up restlessly. 'Let's talk about something else.'

'All right,' said Honor promptly. 'How do you fancy being an aunt?'

Judith rounded on her, eyes wide with astonished delight.

'You mean—already? You're pregnant?'

'Not so much of the already,' said Honor, laughing. 'We've been married for over two months now; a honeymoon baby, to be a bit saccharine.'

Judith hugged her excitedly.

'Who's a clever girl, then. You didn't waste much time, did you!'

'At my age one can't afford to.' Honor returned the hug, then pushed Judith away a little. 'Which brings up my next topic. Martin and I have to be in London next weekend for a charity concert in aid of Famine Relief, you know how involved he is in that sort of thing. A friend of his is lending us his flat in Cadogan Square overnight, and Martin thought you might like to come along for the ride, lend me a bit of support in case I feel peculiar. I do now and again these days.'

Judith regarded her sister's serene face sceptically.

'You look remarkably healthy to me, Honor Gresham. Are you sure all this isn't just part of the campaign for taking little sister's mind off her troubles?'

'It is partly. But Martin's inclined to fly into a panic if I even flutter an eyelid, and why should you spend a lonely Sunday here in Hardwick when you could be in London with us, ready to hold my hand if necessary, which would leave Martin to his duties with an easy mind.' Honor's smile was coaxing.

'I don't know,' said Judith doubtfully. 'I can't help thinking of the last time I came to a concert with you—

pretty disastrous, one way and another. Besides, you know I don't really care for music; not that kind, anyway.'

'This will be all light stuff; you'll enjoy it,' said Honor firmly. 'It will be a change for you, and I'll be glad of company if Martin gets tied up.'

Judith gave in, not because she wanted to go very much, but she knew Honor worried over her. Now she was pregnant it seemed best to humour her, and by the time Honor went home all the details were arranged, even to what dress Judith should wear and who she could change duty with at the hospital.

'By the way, does Mother know about the new arrival?' asked Judith as she saw Honor to her car.

'No. I felt I'd like to get over the queasy morning bit first before making my announcement public—you can imagine how she'll take the news. I'll be knee-deep in advice and baby-clothes before I've had a chance to draw breath.'

'How does Martin feel about it?'

'Ecstatic!'

Judith could well believe it, and waved Honor off, surprised to discover she was envious. She'd never given much thought to children of her own until now, but a sudden picture of having Rafael's child left her wide-eyed and sleepless for most of the night.

The charity concert was to be a gala affair and required Judith's one and only long dress, a conservative black crêpe with long sleeves and a clinging skirt slit to the knee on one side. It had been worn only once before at the Hospital Ball and proved to be a shade looser when Judith tried it on for Honor's approval, but the latter pronounced it perfect for the occasion.

'Is it grand enough for wherever this concert's being held?' asked Judith, eyeing her reflection with doubt.

'Festival Hall, darling, I think, and you look lovely. Wear some beads, or something to liven it up, you look a bit pale lately.'

'Only because I don't get so much fresh air these dark nights—I'll wear some extra blusher if it'll make you happier.'

When Martin came for her on the Sunday morning Judith had to admit it was rather pleasant to be going on a trip. Sundays at home alone tended to drag, and this morning the weather was bright and sunny, so it seemed best to set out to enjoy the unexpected outing to the full. Judith kissed Honor's cheek as she got in the back of the car, smiling at her sister's air of suppressed excitement.

'You look like a little girl out for a special treat, Mrs Gresham.'

Martin grinned as he slid behind the wheel, casting a fond look at his wife's radiant face.

'Pending motherhood suits her, doesn't it.'

'I thought you didn't feel well in the morning, Honor?' said Judith drily.

'Only some mornings, darling!'

They took their time over the journey down, stopping at Oxford for lunch and arriving at the Cadogan Square flat in time for tea. Martin ushered the two women into a large, beautifully-furnished drawing room, and Judith stared round her with appreciation, letting out a low whistle.

'Very nice indeed. Your friend must be loaded, Martin.'

'I don't think he's short of the odd bob or two,' said Martin airily. 'He's not here at the moment, so said I could make use of it. Jolly good of him really. Honor, there'll be all the makings for tea in the kitchen, darling,' he added. 'You put the kettle on and I'll show Judith where she's to sleep.'

There were only two bedrooms, both of them large, and both furnished with the same luxury and taste as the living quarters. Judith examined hers with interest after Martin left her, then unpacked her bag and hung her dress up before joining the others for tea.

Martin had to be at the theatre early, and left the others to follow later rather than subject them to a long wait before curtain up.

'Don't want you bored stiff, Judith,' he said with a grin as he kissed Honor goodbye.

'Don't worry, I promise not to yawn,' she retorted,

'*and* I'll take good care of your wife until you can take over.'

'Not that I need much taking care of tonight,' said Honor, patting her husband's cheek. 'See you later, darling.'

It was a lot later than they expected, both girls a little on edge as their taxi was held up in a snarl of traffic on the way to the theatre.

'Lord, I hope we're not late,' said Judith anxiously.

Honor relaxed as they began to move again. 'Thank goodness. We should just about make it in time now.'

Judith wasn't listening. She was too busy peering through the window trying to make out where they were.

'Honor—are you sure you gave the driver the right address? Even I know the Festival Hall is the other side of the Thames.'

'Yes, darling, it's all right. Actually the concert isn't there after all. I got it wrong.'

Judith frowned at her sister's serene profile, then gave a gasp as the taxi came to a halt near the unmistakable pillared façade of the Royal Opera House. She turned to her sister accusingly.

'You knew it was at Covent Garden all the time! Are you up to something?'

Honor ignored her, occupied with paying the taxi-driver and hurrying a protesting Judith through the doors of the famous lobby, where they were met by Martin. He was frantic.

'Where on earth have you been?' he asked, giving them no time for explanations. 'It's almost eight, put a move on, you two.'

By the time they were all three installed in their seats in the orchestra stalls there was no time for breathless recriminations before the conductor strode to the podium in the orchestra pit to thunderous applause, and after the National Anthem they began to get their breath back to the strains of the overture from *Die Fledermaus*. After this the great velvet curtains with the gold cyphers swept apart to reveal the backdrop for *Swan Lake*, two of the principal dancers posed with the *corps de ballet* ready to dance to Tchaikovsky's famous music. At once Judith relaxed. This, at least, was something she really *did* like, a physical skill and artistry she could relate to and appreciate as she sat back with a sigh of pleasure. Even when the ballet excerpt was followed by a cello solo and a soprano singing an aria from *Faust* Judith was able to give Honor a reassuring smile, indicating she was enjoying the rest of the evening too, anxious to make her sister happy.

In the interval Martin shepherded his two charges to the Crush Bar to drink champagne and meet some of his fellow organisers of the concert. Judith chatted and laughed with people whose names she had difficulty in remembering in the hubbub of conversation going on around her, noticing that three people were pushing through the throng with blithe apologies, obviously making their way in Martin's direction. The man was thin and balding, with sharp intelligent eyes behind dark-rimmed glasses, the twom women with him both beautiful, expensively dressed and with a marked physical resemblance.

'Martin!' The man smiled broadly as he clapped Martin on the shoulder. 'You finally found your ladies—great. Isn't this tremendous? Everyone's in a fever of anticipation. I can't tell you how much this evening means to me.'

'And to me,' said Martin and hurriedly began introductions. 'My wife Honor and my sister-in-law, Judith Russell.'

'I guess Robin should say snap,' smiled the older of the two women. 'I'm Holly Mellor and this is *my* sister, Lenore. Lenore Kramer.'

Judith felt a stab of pain as she smiled and joined in the general amusement at the coincidence. So these were the Mellors, Rafael's agents and such close friends they knew him so much better than she herself could ever hope to now.

'Isn't this just wonderful!' exclaimed Lenore Kramer, in a husky, transatlantic drawl that left no doubt as to her origins, her accent more pronounced than her anglicized sister. She ran slender fingers over her shining hair, the nails painted the exact shade of her elaborate, red-gold coiffure, her long, rather feline green eyes glittering with excitement. 'When Holly gave me the glad news I hopped on the next Concorde—nothing could have kept me away.'

Judith smiled blankly, and glanced at Honor who was fidgeting uneasily. 'What's the matter, love?'

'Nothing,' said Honor hastily, and retreated to the safety of her husband's protective arm.

'I gather you were at Rafael's *last* performance, Miss Russell,' said Holly Mellor, 'so you were one of the fortunate few who heard his swan song. You must be so thrilled to be here at his come-back as well!'

The words took Judith's breath away. She flicked an incredulous, stormy look at Honor and Martin before smiling blandly at the others. 'Oh I am,' she said sweetly. 'Too thrilled for words.'

'How I envy you,' said Lenore dramatically. 'I possess every last one of Rafael's recordings, and just listening to his voice turns my knees to jello, but actually seeing him perform in the flesh—now that's something else.'

Martin coughed, his thin face flushed with embarrassment.

'I'm afraid you've spoilt our surprise.' He cast a hunted glance at his young sister-in-law's stony face. 'I hadn't told Judith we'd be seeing Rafael perform tonight.'

'You mean you didn't know?' Robin Mellor shook his head in disbelief.

'Amazing isn't it?' countered Judith. 'Probably I'm the only one in London who doesn't, or even nationwide. No doubt my parents in Wales are agog with the news at this very minute. Do clear up one point for me, though. Unless someone's discovered some miracle of medicine in Vienna or Switzerland, or somewhere, presumably Rafael won't be singing for us, so what does he intend to do—dance?'

There was much feverish laughter at her sally.

'That's rich,' said Robin Mellor, patting his forehead with a white handkerchief. 'Martin's been playing his cards close to his chest, obviously. Rafael's conducting his own tone poem, Miss Russell. Haven't you seen a programme? Look for yourself.'

Judith studied the large, glossy programme thrust into her hand, unaware of Honor's placatory fingers on her arm. She stared at the item listed as the finale to the concert; a tone poem with the title *Celtic Idyll*, composed and conducted by Rafael David.

'Judith——' said Honor, but Judith barely heard her over the outbreak of animated conversation among the others. The words were in black and white on the thick, shiny paper, unbelievable though they were. This was the bitterest blow of all, and the effort to retain her polite social mask took every last shred of willpower she possessed as she handed the programme back to Robin Mellor and listened to the others going on at length about Rafael's new venture, even agreeing on his strength of character in finding a new outlet for his artistic ability.

'What a man—what an artist!' enthused Lenore. She gave a deprecatory smile and smoothed the clinging jade silk of her dress over her hips. 'Of course, Rafael and I go way back, since before I married my first husband. I've heard Raf sing in most of the opera houses in Europe and Stateside, you know.'

'What enthusiasm, Mrs Kramer. You must be very devoted to music,' said Judith.

'Only when the tenor is sexy as Rafael,' said Holly slyly. 'But you must be fond of music too, Miss Russell?'

'She isn't really,' put in Honor quickly. 'In fact Judith was good enough to come along to keep an eye on me while Martin was busy with the Famine Relief Committee. I'm pregnant,' she announced baldly, flushing as the others exclaimed and congratulated, Lenore cooing over her with extravagance.

Judith stood apart, seared by a deep hurt very close to anger at the thought of Rafael's turning to composing without any hint to her of his intentions. It must obviously mean he no longer felt anything for her, no longer included her in his future plans in any way, or

surely he would have written or telephoned—even a
stupid carnation or two would have been better than
nothing. She went back to her seat with Honor and
Martin, hardly aware of their muted explanations,
brushing them aside with a bright smile as they settled
themselves for the second half of the programme. There
was a *pas-de-deux* from two rising ballet stars,
followed by a tenor singing Puccini and a baritone
singing Mozart, but Judith sat like a waxwork, blind
and deaf to everything but the gradually mounting
wrath inside her. Almost with detachment she considered the idea of simply getting up and walking out of
the Opera House, but rejected the idea regretfully as she
felt Honor's hand close over hers as the applause for
the baritone died away and the great house settled into
an expectant hush as they waited for the man who, all
unknown before to Judith, the majority of the audience
had really paid to see.

When the tall, familiar figure in unfamiliar white tie
and tails finally appeared, threading his way through
the orchestra to step up on to the podium the applause
that greeted him was deafening. Judith swallowed hard,
staring with overt hunger at Rafael's grave face for an
instant as he bowed and acknowledged the tumultuous
reception. She shrank down into her seat, instinctive in
her desire to hide, knowing she was ridiculous, yet
almost certain that for a moment his eyes had found her
before he turned his back and lifted the baton. In utter
silence the audience waited before the first melancholy
sound of the oboe responded to the coaxing baton,
which beckoned the other instruments to follow suit,
section by section, the rest of the woodwinds, then the
strings and brass all woven together in the mounting
excitement of the opening theme until finally the great
roll of the tympani heralded a change of mood, the
entire orchestra responding to Rafael's expressive hands
and lithe body, which moved like a physical expression
of the music he drew from the musicians, a melody
of haunting serenity gradually mounting again to a
joyous paean of triumph and joy which rose to a heart-
stopping climax of sensual sound at Rafael's imperious

command, then died away little by little until only the
mournful oboe was left alone to shiver into silence that
lasted a full five seconds before the audience erupted
into wild applause and shouts of 'bravo' from all over
the house.

Judith let out the breath she had been holding, sitting
perfectly still as she stared up at Rafael. He was
breathing hard as he took his bow, then brought the
orchestra to their feet to take theirs. She watched him
with bleak irony, feeling like some humble mortal
looking up at a god on the heights of Mount Olympus.
The figure up there was some glittering stranger from
another world; nothing to do with Judith Russell at all.
Summoning a smile she turned to Honor and Martin
after Rafael left the rostrum.

'Thank you for bringing me,' she said simply,
meaning every word. 'I wouldn't have missed it for the
world.'

'Sorry about all the cloak and dagger stuff,' said
Martin awkwardly.

'You know you wouldn't have come otherwise,'
added Honor.

Judith managed a laugh.

'Dead right I wouldn't. And just see what I'd have
missed. But I'd very much like to get out of here now, if
you don't mind, and get back to the flat.'

'But you can't do that!' Honor looked aghast.
'There's a supper-party, Judith, with Rafael as guest of
honour, and you're invited, and——'

'Honor,' said Judith, with a dangerous wobble in her
voice, 'just what are you trying to do to me? I'm not
thick, you know. I'm fairly sure I'm getting Rafael's
message, loud and clear, and it says "over and out", so
just let me go—*please*!'

Nothing Honor and Martin could say would move
her, nor would she let them go with her. Martin's place
was at the party anyway, in his capacity of committee
member, and Honor's place was with him Judith stated
with such finality there was no more argument, except
that Martin made sure he installed Judith safely in a
taxi before letting her go back to the flat alone.

Left to herself at last Judith was hard put to keep back the tears on the journey. She gritted her teeth and stared out at the passing lights until she arrived at Cadogan Square and finally gained sanctuary inside the flat. She went straight through to the bedroom and threw her velvet wrap on the bed, almost tempted to throw herself down as well, but she resisted the impulse and made for the bathroom to splash cold water on her burning cheeks. She stared at her stormy face in the mirror, her brain reeling from the excess of emotion experienced during the evening, a shaming jealousy of Lenore Kramer and all she represented warring with the bitter hurt dealt by Rafael in his silence about his new career. Without doubt there were Lenore Kramers everywhere Rafael performed, only too eager to provide whatever form of diversion he required—Rafael himself had admitted he had never been neglected, after all. How stupid she had been even to imagine she could compete. Only until tonight she had never thought of competing in this particular sphere, nor considered the strength and quality of the competition. Lenore Kramer and Holly Mellor had both been wearing model gowns, probably from designers like Bill Blass or Bruce Oldfield. Judith gave a mirthless little laugh. Her own sober little black dress had been bought off the peg at a department store in Birmingham, quite expensive in fact, but certainly not exclusive. She shook her head, puzzled over Martin and Honor's reasons for bringing her to London for the concert in the first place. Knowing them both it had no doubt been for the best of reasons, but, Lord, what an experience it had turned out to be; painful in the extreme, but illuminating. At least she now had things in perspective. In Wales, away from everything, Judith Russell and Rafael David had been two people who came together in equality, the only difference between them the joyous one of their sex. Now they were well and truly back in their pigeon-holes again; Judith the small town physiotherapist, and Rafael the international star, regardless of whether he were singing, composing, conducting or whatever. And never the twain should meet again if she had anything to do with it.

Judith rubbed her temples wearily, almost fancying she could still hear Rafael's music running through her brain. Suddenly she stiffened. She *could* hear it, very quietly, certainly, but from somewhere close at hand, not inside her own head. Then it stopped and she shook herself irritably. Hallucinations she could do without. Coffee. That was the answer. Judith crossed the hall to the kitchen, but stopped dead in her tracks outside the closed drawing-room door. The music had started up again, bringing up the hairs on the back of her neck, and it wasn't the piece heard at the Opera House either. Musical ignoramus she might be, but this music was something she recognised with a shiver of reminiscence, even though heard only once before. It was from the opera *La Rondine*, and she had heard Rafael sing it on the stage of the William Gresham Theatre on a never-to-be forgotten evening not so very long ago.

Judith clenched her teeth and stared at the closed door, common sense assuring her a burglar intent on breaking and entering would hardly stop to enjoy a record on her host's stereo system. Then without warning every last drop of blood in her body threatened to drain away as an unmistakable voice rose above the orchestra, the pure golden sound bringing hot tears to Judith's eyes as the liquid, impassioned notes poured out in pleading. Even though the pleading was in Italian she knew very well what the words meant, not only from Rafael's perfect diction, but from much secret poring over the libretto translation during the restless days after her first meeting with him.

'No! Rimani! Non lasciarmi solo!' implored his voice, repeating the phrase with a cadence of such despair it tore Judith apart. Then abruptly there was silence again and she summoned up her forces, opening the door and snapping on the light as she stormed into the room.

'What do you think you're doing . . .' Judith trailed lamely into silence. The room was empty, the only sign of life the tiny red light on the expensive stereo. Baffled, Judith threw an uneasy look over her shoulder, then irritably she crossed the large room to turn off the stereo, almost jumping out of her skin as the music began once more. The tape had re-started itself. This time Judith waited, scowling, her foot tapping angrily as the sequence of music and pauses ran its length, concluding as before with Rafael's voice pleading with her to stay, not to leave him alone. Grimly Judith heard him out, then switched off the stereo and pulled it away from the wall to discover it was attached to a small computer on the floor.

'Well, well, well,' murmured Judith aloud. 'The miracles of modern science. And just how did that get there, I wonder?'

'I put it there,' said an amused voice behind her, and Judith flung round to see Rafael leaning indolently in the doorway, a key-ring swinging from one finger.

A great flood of angry colour washed over Judith's face and receded, leaving her colourless with fury. 'What are *you* doing here?' she demanded, consumed with a fierce desire to lash out at him as he lounged there, no longer the formal stranger in evening dress, but more like the man she knew, casual in sweater and slacks, a leather jacket slung over his shoulders.

'I live here,' he said casually. 'When I am in London, that is. It is my apartment.'

Judith strugged to keep her temper under control. 'Martin said it belonged to a friend,' she snapped.

'I am his friend, no?'

'He said the friend was away.'

'Alas, he was compelled to lie. I am not away. I am here,' said Rafael, the gleam in his eyes belying his gravity.

Judith glared at him. 'And is this where you've been all the time?'

'No. After—after I left you, Judith, I drove to Granada. I did not know where else to go. And all the time I was driving there I hear—heard this music in my brain.' He moved from the doorway, advancing a little towards her, his eyes unwavering as they held her. 'I was desolated, Judith. This music I heard was not happy, either, yet it seemed to ease my melancholy a little, almost to illustrate it, and when I finally reached Casa de las Flores I sat down at the piano and I played the tune in my brain, and it grew. It became the musical expression of the brief, beautiful time we spent together at Morfa, all the sadness and the great, burning happiness I experienced when you were there with me. Did you not hear all this in the music tonight, Judith?'

She shook her head. 'No. The music was very atmospheric, but all I could think of was that you wrote it without telling me, and you were actually here in this country without letting me know. To me it seemed to be telling me I was extraneous, quite definitely not part of this new life of yours.'

'What you are saying is that I wanted you when things were bad for me, then when they were not so bad I just discarded you.' Rafael's eyes flamed for a moment before his thick lashes dropped to hide them. 'Your opinion does not flatter, *chica*.'

Judith shrugged indifferently. 'Shouldn't you be at a party now? I heard you were guest of honour.'

'It will still function without me,' he said calmly. 'I wished you to be there with me. You did not, so I came here.'

'Mrs Kramer will be disappointed,' said Judith rashly.

'Lenore?' Rafel's eyes narrowed. 'You have met her tonight?'

'Yes.' Judith's chin lifted. 'She said you were old friends from "way back".'

'I have known her a long time, yes. It is natural—she is related to one of my agents. I have known many people for a long time. And you for only a short time. Does it make a difference?'

'No. I suppose not.' Judith's eyes veered away from his. 'How did Honor and Martin come into all the fun and games tonight?'

'I asked them to bring you here to London, to drag you to the concert by force if necessary.' Rafael's voice was harsh. 'I thought you would be glad. So did they. Martin said you were unhappy without me. I appears we were all wrong—about everything.'

Judith was silent. Tears formed at the corners of her

eyes and began to run down her cheeks. 'You weren't wrong,' she said at last, in a choked voice. 'I didn't know—didn't realise——'

'That my music was a gift for you, Judith? I wanted to do something which would merit your love, to show I earned our life together. But, being the performer I am I wanted to put on a show for you.' Rafael made no move, but his voice softened and grew husky, and Judith looked up at him, sniffing, still angry about the weeks of silence and misery; yet bound up with the anger, like a bright thread of gold, was the certain knowledge that here in front of her, his eyes glittering like citrines under the slanting brows, was the only man she ever wanted, ever would want, beyond all possible doubt. But the urge to punish lingered, and she resisted the yearning to hurl herself into his arms, wanting him to suffer a little, not only for his silence, but for fraying her emotions with such an emotive reminder of his superb voice.

'You frightened me,' she said flatly, eyeing him with resentment as she gestured to the stereo. 'Your gadgetry scared me out of my wits.'

'Scared of a little music? You, Judith?' He was openly laughing at her. 'My intrepid Amazon? Never!'

'I thought someone had broken in until I discovered your computer.'

'Ingenious, no? I have a friend in the recording business who showed me what to do. One simply puts an interface into the——'

'Spare me the technicalities, Rafael.' Judith turned away and sat down on a sofa. 'I presume you set it all up before I arrived today.'

Rafael came nearer and stood looking down at her.

'Yes, I did. Then I had Martin turn it on. My plan was to make only a token appearance at the party with you, then bring you back here, and if my competence as a composer and conductor had not softened you towards me I hoped the words on the tape would achieve it. That was why I installed it—for the words. Did you understand them, Judith?'

'Oh yes,' she admitted, turning away. 'I know what they meant.'

'To be honest I had hopes that if all else failed you might be softened by hearing the voice I once had.' Rafael sat down beside her, but made no move to touch her. 'Did it strike any chord in you, Judith? You know I was saying "stay, do not leave me alone".'

'Ah, but how alone is alone, Rafael?' She gave him a glinting sidelong look. 'Tonight I gained quite a fair idea of how much consolation could be available to you.'

He lifted one shoulder expressively.

'I am asking you to share my life, Judith, not just my bed.' He caught her chin in one hand and turned her face to his. 'What else must I do before you say yes, *chica? Dios*—you are hard on me!'

'*I'm* hard on *you*?' she cried passionately. 'How do you think I've felt all this time without a word? And while we're on the subject, why were you so aloof and distant at Honor's wedding, even afterwards when we went to the car alone together?'

'Because then, *querida*, I was not sure I would have success as a composer, and because then I was not certain of the success of another plan which is now certainty.' Suddenly he turned and seized her by the elbows. 'I was exerting great self-control all the time not to pull you into my arms and kiss you senseless, little fool. But it was, after all, your sister's wedding. Not an occasion to mar with such unrestrained behaviour.' He shook her slightly. 'And do not forget, Judith Russell, that *I* was the one who was rejected!'

Judith looked at him, doubt in her wide, dark eyes.

'I know,' she said with difficulty, and tried half-heartedly to free herself.

'No. I shall not let you go.' Rafael moved nearer, the familiar, pulse-quickening scent of him in her nostrils as he drew her gently towards him. 'Do not pull away. I have something of importance to tell you.'

Abruptly Judith was tired of words. She raised eyes lambent with invitation and said huskily, 'Tell me later,' putting up her hands to bring his face down to hers. 'I've been so wretched, Rafael. I'm very glad your music was successful tonight, but in some ways it doesn't matter to me. Nothing matters if I'm honest, nothing except to be with you, wherever you are, whatever you want to do or not do. If—if you still want me, that is.'

Rafael cast his eyes heavenwards and shook her quite roughly. '*Dios*—what else must I do to prove it?'

Judith slid her arms round him and raised her mouth. 'You could kiss me.'

His eyes kindled and his mouth met hers in a passion of tenderness and relief as he lifted her on to his lap and cradled her against him, his hands caressing her gently while his mouth moved over her face feature by feature, as though to memorise her all over again by touch.

'Ah, *linda flor*,' he sighed at last. 'How I have longed to hold you in my arms like this again. My heart and my very soul have longed for you.'

An uncontrollable giggle shook Judith and she raised a teasing face to his. 'Your rather extravagant use of the English language takes a little getting used to, my darling!'

He stared down at her with hauteur. 'I say only what I feel.'

She nodded lovingly and settled back into his embrace. 'Yes. I'm beginning to realise that. But don't imagine I've forgiven you yet for frightening me with that wicked contraption of yours. I genuinely thought I was being haunted by your voice, you great ham.'

'Ham? That is something to eat, no?'

'M'm. Like this.' Delicately she began to nibble along his jawline with tantalising slowness until he turned blindly to find her mouth with his and there was no more talking for some time until, with a tremendous effort, Rafael raised his head.

'No,' he said, breathless and flushed, but determined. 'First I must tell you what else I have been doing since we parted.'

'Since you walked out on me, you mean!'

'You think it was easy to do?' Rafael's face was austere with the memory. 'Yet afterwards at the Casa de las Flores in Granada, I was almost grateful to you.'

'Oh, really!'

'I said "almost", *mi amor*, not entirely.' His arms tightened as he looked possessively at her face against his shoulder. 'But you were right. A life of lotus-eating, as you described it, would not content either you or me—I? No matter. So. Not only did you give me inspiration to compose my *Celtic Idyll*, but after a while I thought of something else to occupy my time now I cannot sing.'

'You're going to conduct!' Judith sat up, her eyes shining. 'You looked so fantastic on that podium, Rafael. You'd be a natural at conducting opera, surely, with all your experience on the stage?'

'I have thought of it,' he agreed, with a brilliant smile at her enthusiasm. 'Having been a singer I feel I could conduct opera with a special sympathy for the singers and the musicians—but I wander from the point. My good idea is to found a school for young opera singers, whether they can pay or not. I have the house. I have money, and I have friends. Bryn Tudor, for one, is willing to come in on it with me. He will devote some time to coaching, and can put up a little money. I'm sure others will contribute some time also, and of course I shall take master-classes myself. I shall enjoy that, I think.'

'That's a wonderful idea,' exclaimed Judith. 'But what about me?'

'I shall enjoy you, too, *mi corazón*,' he said huskily and kissed her hard.

'That's not what I meant.' Face scarlet she pulled away. 'I just wondered if you could use another recruit?'

Rafael eyed her up and down, pretending to consider. 'It is possible, of course, that I could have need of a physiotherapist—possibly I can think of a job for you.'

Judith pushed her tumbling hair from her face. 'Would the pay be good?'

Rafael lifted a shoulder, an evil glint in his eye. 'No. But there would be fringe benefits I think you say.'

'Oh yes. Such as?'

'You would have to keep the Maestro happy, do what he commands at all times.'

'Commands!'

'Implores!' Without warning Rafael slid to his knees in front of Judith, hands clasped together in ultra dramatic plea. 'Say you will be mine forever, *querida*, do not destroy my life with your refusal, I beg——'

'For heaven's sake shut up, you idiot!' Judith threw a cushion at him with such force he landed flat on his back, laughing helplessly. 'If that's an opera libretto no wonder they don't sing them in English very often!'

Rafael sat up and clasped his hands round his knees, sober again, his eyes questioning. 'Will you, Judith? Are you willing to spend your life with musicians? I can do nothing else—my whole life has been music.'

'I've already found out how little choice I have,' she said candidly. 'Without you life turned out to be pretty meaningless anyway. So if I need to work I'll practice my skills on your pupils, make them fitter. You can build a gymnasium where I can put them through their paces.'

'Anything you wish, *amada*.'

'Then I very much fear you're stuck with me!'

'I have no fear.' Rafael's smile faded. 'I *was* afraid, Judith. But now I have you back I shall never fear anything again.'

Judith's eyes were soft with compassion.

'What were you afraid of, Rafael? Of not being able to sing anymore?'

'No. I had come to terms with that before you came to Brynmorfa. It was only after I had a taste of what life could be with you at my side that I found the prospect of life without you so terrifying.'

They stared at each other gravely for a moment, then Rafael put out a hand to touch Judith's.

'What is it?' she whispered.

'It is just that my beautiful girl has recovered her glow. The light is burning inside you once more, unlike the creature I met at the wedding—so elegant, so *soignée*, but so lifeless. Nothing at all like that vivid, flying figure I first met in the park.'

'Mowed down,' she said indignantly, then sighed. 'Oh

Rafael, it's been such hell without you. I thought you'd lost interest in me after Honor's wedding.'

'But then, I am good at pretending. I have made my living by my talent for pretending, Judith.' Rafael stayed where he was on the floor, his face alight with passionate sincerity. 'But I pretend nothing now, Judith. I love you, I want you, and I pray you feel the same about me. Do you, little one?'

Judith smiled shakily. 'You know very well I do.'

Wordlessly Rafael held up his arms and she slid down into them with a sigh of pure happiness, surrendering herself to his mouth and hands with rapture, only stirring when something occurred to her.

'Let me up, Rafael, we can't stay here like this, Honor and Martin will be here any time.'

He shook his head, eyes dancing, and pulled her back into his arms. 'I engaged a room for them at the Savoy.'

'You did what!' Judith stared at him in astonishment. 'What on earth did they think—not to mention the utter extravagance!'

'They will think we need time to be alone. Martin understands only too well that given the choice I would have had you safely married to me long since; so does Honor. And I know they approve.' He raised himself on one elbow to look down with pleasure at her flushed face. 'Besides, I consider they deserve some reward for all their help in getting you to London and keeping my secret, no? Poor Honor found it all most difficult—she wanted so very much to tell you everything.'

'Poor darling, it must have been agony for her.'

'Then you agree my extravagance was justified. Speaking for myself no price is too high to pay for a night spent in your arms, *amada*.'

Judith dissolved into helpless giggles. 'You can't say that—it's disreputable!'

Rafael chuckled as he stretched himself full length beside her. 'You know very well what I mean, little tease. Take great care, or I shall exact my revenge when you begin learning Spanish.'

'I'll keep you to that. In the meantime may I ask a question?'

'Anything, *querida*.'

'I just wondered why we're lying on this tastefully carpeted but frankly hard floor, when there are two unoccupied beds across the hall.' She smiled at him demurely.

'An excellent question.' Rafael jumped up, laughing, and pulled Judith to her feet. 'As long as you mean one of them to remain unoccupied, of course.'

'You bet your sweet life I do,' said Judith emphatically, gathering up her long skirt in one hand. 'I'll race you——'

'No, *chica*,' he swung her up into his arms, kissing her smiling mouth. 'Let me carry you, then I can do this on the way. Better, no?'

Judith rubbed her cheek against his in enthusiastic agreement.

'Very much better. Only the word's "yes", Rafael, "yes."

Harlequin Presents

Coming Next Month

879 THAI TRIANGLE Jayne Bauling
In Thailand an artist tries to bring two brothers together before it's too late. In love with one, she can't break her promise to the other—not even to avoid heartache.

880 PILLOW PORTRAITS Rosemary Carter
An assignment to ghostwrite a famous artist's autobiography seems like the chance of a lifetime—until he insists on her baring her soul, too, even her deepest secret.

881 DARK DREAM Daphne Clair
When her childhood sweetheart brings home a fiancée, a young woman finds herself marrying a widower who claims to love her. Yet he still dreams about his first wife!

882 POINT OF IMPACT Emma Darcy
On a ferry in Sydney Harbour it is a night to celebrate. Although the man she once loved is present, a model throws caution to the wind and announces her engagement. The shockwaves are immediate!

883 INJURED INNOCENT Penny Jordan
Co-guardians are at loggerheads—not so much over their differing views on how to raise the little girls as over an unresolved conflict from the past.

884 DANGER ZONE Madeleine Ker
An English fashion designer in New York is drawn to a successful merchant banker, despite his disturbing, reckless streak and the strain it places on their love.

885 SWEET AS MY REVENGE Susan Napier
The owner of an Australian secretarial agency is trapped and forced to face the consequences of her foolhardy act to save her brother's career. But no one tricks her into falling in love.

886 ICE INTO FIRE Lilian Peake
When her parents' marriage shatters, a young woman vows never to be burned by love. But at a Swiss chalet, a man who equally mistrusts emotion manages to melt her resolve.

Available in May wherever paperback books are sold, or through Harlequin Reader Service.

In the U.S.
P.O. Box 1397
Buffalo, N.Y.
14240-1397

In Canada
P.O. Box 2800, Postal Station A
5170 Yonge Street
Willowdale, Ontario M2N 6J3

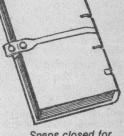

Can you keep a secret?

You can keep this one plus 4 free novels

WORLDWIDE LIBRARY IS YOUR TICKET TO ROMANCE, ADVENTURE AND EXCITEMENT

Experience it all in these big, bold Bestsellers— Yours exclusively from WORLDWIDE LIBRARY WHILE QUANTITIES LAST

To receive these Bestsellers, complete the order form, detach and send together with your check or money order (include 75¢ postage and handling), payable to WORLDWIDE LIBRARY, to:

In the U.S.
WORLDWIDE LIBRARY
901 Fuhrmann Blvd.
Buffalo, N.Y. 14269

In Canada
WORLDWIDE LIBRARY
P.O. Box 2800, 5170 Yonge Street
Postal Station A, Willowdale, Ontario
M2N 6J3

Quant.	Title	Price
_____	WILD CONCERTO, Anne Mather	$2.95
_____	A VIOLATION, Charlotte Lamb	$3.50
_____	SECRETS, Sheila Holland	$3.50
_____	SWEET MEMORIES, LaVyrle Spencer	$3.50
_____	FLORA, Anne Weale	$3.50
_____	SUMMER'S AWAKENING, Anne Weale	$3.50
_____	FINGER PRINTS, Barbara Delinsky	$3.50
_____	DREAMWEAVER, Felicia Gallant/Rebecca Flanders	$3.50
_____	EYE OF THE STORM, Maura Seger	$3.50
_____	HIDDEN IN THE FLAME, Anne Mather	$3.50
_____	ECHO OF THUNDER, Maura Seger	$3.95
_____	DREAM OF DARKNESS, Jocelyn Haley	$3.95

	YOUR ORDER TOTAL	$_____
	New York and Arizona residents add appropriate sales tax	$_____
	Postage and Handling	$___.75
	I enclose	$_____

NAME _____

ADDRESS _____ APT.# _____

CITY _____

STATE/PROV. _____ ZIP/POSTAL CODE _____

WW-1-3

What the press says about Harlequin romance fiction...

"When it comes to romantic novels...
Harlequin is the indisputable king."
— *New York Times*

"...always with an upbeat, happy ending."
— *San Francisco Chronicle*

"Women have come to trust these
stories about contemporary people,
set in exciting foreign places."
— *Best Sellers*, New York

"The most popular reading matter of
American women today."
— *Detroit News*

"...a work of art."
— *Globe & Mail*, Toronto

Take 4 novels and a surprise gift FREE